HOMELESS AND BROKEN

BY

BONNY FRANKE

Homeless and Broken

ISBN

Paperback: 978-1-77419-071-5

Ebook: 978-1-77419-076-0

MAPLE LEAF PUBLISHING INC.

3rd Floor 4915 54 St Red Deer,

Alberta T4N 2G7 Canada

General Inquiries & Customer Service

Phone: 1-(403)-356-0255

Toll Free: 1-(888)-498-9380

Email: info@mapleleafpublishinginc.com

Contents

Characters

Blondie – homeless

Sam – tall black man

Barry – ex navy seal with no lower legs or feet

Darcy – black gay woman

Willie – short, round man with scooter

Mr. Fields – Blondie's friend

Woman – Wears Salvation Army shirt

Jewel – waitress

Ella – small child

Bella – Sturdy Housekeeper

Amelia Margot – Bella's sister

Tommy – almost a year old boy

Dr. Cooper - Amelia Margot's doctor

Extras:

Hostess in restaurant

Crowd in restaurant

Bad boy – four _________ teens

Older woman in library

Man in gas station

Young woman in library

__________ homeless at food dine

Servers at food dine

Two servers at Ree Center

Homeless at Ree Center

3 Policemen

4 Firemen

Crowd of Orientals

Man with boom box

Woman who yelled

Volunteer – Ella's mother

2 pilgrims they followed

Nurse – in Dr. Hamilton's office

Dr. Hamilton

Mrs. Sinclair – Tommy's mother

Clyde Porter – Blondie's teacher friend

CHAPTER 1

BLONDIE

Dust devils swirl. Loneliness continues. Phone rings from afar. Nothing absolves the pain. There is a difference in being broke and in being poor. Broke means having no money. Poor means no soul to make things happen. Being poor means somebody's git up and go, got up and left.

She didn't know who she was talking to. She was just talking. More muttering to herself. She was not even talking out loud.

That's the way Poor sets in. Some say "down and out." Yessiree, down plus out. Out of caring or wantin to do more they they want to do.

Some folks get Poor and some folks get Broke. Some folks get Broken or different. I happen to be one of those folks who get Broken and Broke. Then they get Poor.

 Still, no one eases the pain.

I don't know if I should cry or laugh. Don't know. Can't see well. My eyes usta be okay. Maybe one is just swollen shut. The boys yesterday (or was it before then?) sure did a number on my face.

One eye feels bruised. Swollen. Just a squint, maybe. Bet it is black or blue. (giggles) Usta be blue on the inside at least.

Seeing well is not always required. Listening is required. Hearing is not enough. Have to listen in order to be heard.

Had a mirror once. Probably broke. At least can't see the black or green where those boys hit on me. Musta broke my nose, too. Sure did bleed down my front. Why'd they do what they did? Don't know. Musta wanted sex.

No! No! No! How many times do I have to say No! Can you not hear? Do you not know the word? No means NO! Leave me alone!

Oh goodie. Hit at two. What? Do you need four bad ones to do your job for you? Oh there's only three of your buddies standing guard. Okay. So. You're the big man! Now go away! You're nothing but a street punk!

Ohhhhhhh. Some tall stranger came by from nowhere. He was bigger than the biggest of the street punks. The leader of the street gang tried to get my jeans down. Thank goodness they were tight!

After the stranger showed up, I managed to roll to the curb. That's when the dry heaves started. They just came from nowhere and produced nothing. Had to eat before could produce anything. Must eat.

From the curb, could see his coat pulled back. Had a gun stuck under his belt. Guess that made the bad boys go away. He musta gone away too. Don't know. Too busy trying to throw up.

Don't like guns. Scared of guns. Guns hurt people. Punches hurt. Rips, pulls, pushes hurt. My only blouse now tattered. Shoving, being pushed around or aside.

Seems like its common some days. Moving around hurts all ever. It's hard. Concrete is hard, too. Can't lie here much longer. Need real sleep. Must leave. Can't run. Still, must run.

Run? That's silly... guess I'll just wander around a while until I get my feet back under me. Can't help but wonder who that tall guy was. He sure did appear all of a sudden.

Once, seems a long time ago, had a job. Taught literature. Read all those books. Books or plays by Albee. Albee, who's he?

Read Cather...she's hard... Thoreau, Melville. Maybe even Eliot. He had initials instead of a name.

Might have been...don't know. Some letters won't stay put if they are just in my head. Guess I'll have to write them down if I am s'posed to remember them. Oh, no. Can't write 'em down. Nuthin' to write on! No paper and stuff. Ha. Cracked another funny. Must be gathering myself.

Ha! Even read Shakespeare. "To have or not to have" – that's a joke. Had, now it is gone. So, I guess it is... We have not! Oh, well.

Too much thinking about yesterday's hurts the head. Must go. Wish there was some place to go to. Wish there was a nickel for every book I read. Wish there was a nickel in my pocket. Wishing won't do any good to anybody. If wishing worked, there would be so many wishes floating around there would be barely enough air to breathe.

Guess I hafta sit and rest now. Sit? That's a joke too. Where's to sit? Guess I'll just lean against a pole. Surely could have walked more than a couple blocks. Feel like an old well-used punching bag.

Oh look! A radio. Somebody musta tossed out an old radio. Wonder if it works. Better look around. See if anybody is close by. Better grab it. See if it works before any snatcher comes around.

Head hurts. Bad, but not like... hope it's not more of those strange things they took out of my head last time. Don't want to go through that again.

Oh yeah. One station comes on. Lots of static. A man says 'Good Morning'. He hasn't seen me, that's a joke for sure! Don't think it's such a good morning. Then he has to go and say a 'chance of rain'! Don't want rain either.

So what if I'm dirty. Nobody cares anyway. Head sure does hurt. Can't hear much for all that static. Guess I'll put the radio in my pushcart, if I know where my cart went. Boys could have made off with it.

Seem to be wood. The radio, not my head. Wish my head were wood. Might not hurt so bad, plus they could yell, 'Come on, Wooden Head'.

Yeah. That's a good one. They could call me Wooden Head instead of Amelia, or Melly, or even Amy like they sometimes do. Plus, they may even stop pulling my hair just because it's longer than it was. Usta be blond. Now it's mostly dirty. Maybe grey. Don't know.

Had some hair cut out. Should say 'cut off'. Don't know which is best. Also don't know who 'they' are. Besides, don't know where they took me afterwards. Do remember they picked me up then somebody laid me on a rolling cart. It was warm. Felt good.

Slept a lot. Good, warm sleep. Almost woke up once. Heard a voice say, "Don't know what this is. Never saw anything like it before. It surely is long. Oh, well. We'll keep going".

They... whoever they were... musta kept going. I don't know. Slept for days, or weeks, or months maybe. Whatever. Sure was good and seems like they tried to wake me up. All I wanted to do was sleep. Musta been months and months. Seemed like a long time. One was slapping my arm. Another was slapping my cheek. It was too much.

Musta woke up. Had tubes and needles everywhere. Hears some-one calling "Mama" Musta been me.

"Your Mama is gone," someone said.

"It's okay. She'll be back." I know that was me.

"No. She's gone. She's dead."

They tried to convince me. I didn't listen.

Dreams taunt sleep still. Can't seem to make them go away. Some are not so bad. Others are too bad to finish.

Yesterday dreamed of a gang of boys. They'd cornered a little girl and beat up on her. She'd been kicked, tossed, bitten and bleeding everywhere. Oh, God! Made myself wake up.

Some bad dreams are kinda like books. Some should never be printed. They're not even any good for toilet paper.

Oh no. Shouldn't think that. Sure am glad nobody knows what I'm thinking.

CHAPTER 2

SAM

There's Sam. Must have a real name. Maybe his name is Samuel. He will know where there's something to eat. Not the garbage cans again! There's rats in most. Don't like rats.

"Hey, Sam. Where you gonna eat? Gotta eat."

"Whoa, Blondie. You look a mess. You fall again? Did somebody do you, or at least tried?"

"I'm okay. Just some stuff on my best shirt. I'll brush it off. Gotta eat. Where you going?"

"Come on. Ah'll show ya. Besides, that brown stuff looks like blood to me. It won't brush off ya know."

"Oh dear. You got a spare shirt I can borrow? Gotta eat, you know. My good shirt is only fit for the trash right now"

Sam rifled through his worn backpack and pulled out an old wrinkled plaid shirt. He handed it over while Blondie shed her other shirt. The plaid shirt came down past her knees. She giggled while she rolled up the sleeves past her grimy hands.

"Look!" She twittered. "I'm covered up! Can't tell if I'm a female or not. I'll just pull my plait... or is it a braid... out of the collar. There. Guess it will do just fine."

Sam laughed at the big shirt on the small woman. He was glad he had a spare even though it looked funnier than she did with the 'brown stuff' all over her.

"Can we go someplace to eat now? Gotta eat now."

Sam sook his thin brown head and said, "Sure. Come on."

They trudged several blocks then turned a corner to a Soup Kitchen that was open all day for those who wanted and needed food. Cheers, whistles, catcalls, and claps from many of those already seated followed the duo inside. Some of the others ignored them both

Sam and Blondie tried to ignore the clammer as they headed toward a slow-moving line.

"Hey there, Sam!"

He waved behind his head as he pushed Blondie in front of him.

"Who you got there?" he heard. "A boy-friend with long stringy hair? What the matter with his face? You have to beat him up?"

A voice came from someone who had finished but was still chomping on bread.

"Yawl hush!" Sam turned toward the folks who were yelling. "Ain't no boy. No. I didn't ruff 'em up! Gotta git food now, so hush up!"

Sam's tall demeanor and harsh voice quieted the rabble rouser but some mumbled to each other while most stayed quiet.

"I know you're well known around these parts. But why are they being mean?"

"Don't pay them no mind. Go on now. The line seems to be movin'. Let's git somethun to eat."

Blondie fumbled with her spoon then hurried to find a vacant bench and table on which to eat. She emptied her bowl by drinking it while managing to spill a lot down her front. Her busted and swollen lip didn't slow her down.

Sam watched her as he quietly spooned soup through his broken teeth.

"Can I get more?" Blondie asked.

"Sho nuff. Get in that mostly empty line there," Sam said in a low voice. "You gotta wait yo turn til they hand you some."

Blondie wasted no time hurrying toward the stragglers who waited in front of her. As soon as she could she held out her empty bowl.

"Please," she murmured.

A volunteer server shook his head but said nothing as he took her bowl and ladled more soup into it. He held a piece of cornbread with long tongs out to her. She grabbed the bread, tuckered her face downward and grinned as she bunched her shoulders.

Almost running but afraid she'd spill her soup; she made her way back to where Sam sat patiently.

"Oh my. This is good," Blondie murmured with her head still down. She bent over the warm liquid, almost afraid it would be snatched away,

Sam began to straddle the bench he was on. "Gotta go." He stretched up to his full size, well over six feet, four inches. Blondie felt the table scoot as he got ready to leave.

With her bowl almost empty, she looked up at him and hesitantly asked, "Where you going?"

"Gotta check on sumpthin."

Blondie hurriedly drank the rest of the rest of the soup and tried to jump up to follow Sam. She got the long shirttail tangled in the bench as she tried to move too fast. Tears began to form in her eyes as she called out.

"Sam. Wait. I remember. I remember finally finding the school or college or whatever it was. Sam. Do you hear me? I remember." Tears ran down her face.

Sam stopped. He turned toward her and waited.

She wrung her hands then untangled the long shirt from the bench. Almost falling in her haste, she blurted softly so that only Sam could hear her, she stood in front of the tall man with tears streaking her face.

"I remember. Don't you see? It just now came to me. I remember the President. He sat at a big rolltop desk and had on a dark suit with pinstripes. He turned toward me and said something about... I don't know what. It musta been something about all the surgeries I'd had on my head. Maybe it was about my classes, or something. But don't you see? I remembered him."

Sam waited. He stood still as tears washed down her bruised face.

"I remember he said I wouldn't have any classes any more. Why'd he say that, Sam? Mama was dead, he said. But I remember Melville's *The Old Man and the Sea.* 'Call me Ishmael'. Why'd he say I couldn't teach?"

She put both hands over her face. Sam walked toward her. She cried.

"Hush now. It's alright now," Sam whispered, "Come on. Let's walk some. You ate. Let's go. Don't want the folks in here to know anything they can't make up. Come on." He waited.

Blondie brushed tears from her face and stumbled toward his outstretched hand. He caught her as she tried to reach toward him.

"Time to go," he said as he held up his bony hand with the palm toward the main heckler to stop any smart comments. They hushed.

The half-filled room was quiet as they went out. Even the servers behind the counter held their ladles and were stock still. All the sound was gone except for Blondie's occasional hiccup.

Sam held open the door for Blondie. She stopped outside and looked up at him. "Where are we going, Sam?"

He didn't say anything but kept walking with his hands in his pockets, shaking his head.

They walked; he was in front. Went past a few huddled doorways. She shuffled behind him.

"So," he said, "You remembered. So what, you're here now. So what! Gotta use all that book learning now!" They walked some more, in silence. He stopped, "You can't keep following me around, I got things to do!"

"Well Boo Hoo! I 'member things now!" she picked at her swollen lower lip, winced, and stood straighter. "I remember Mama too."

Sam turned and looked at her with his hands on his hips, "So, she dead. You remember that, too? So what! Leave me alone!"

Scolding made her stand still. She wrapped the long shirt closer around herself, stopped crying, and stared at Sam. She turned to walk away, defiant, then whipped around.

"Mama's dead?" Blondie stopped, Stared off to nowhere. "Mama's big. She's strong. She's dead? Don't remember that!"

Sam walked toward her. Looked down at Blondie. Knew she was off somewhere else. He started to slap her but checked his hand.

Blondie was trying. He waited.

"Musta been when they took me to a hospital someplace. Nobody told me, she'd go around holding her hand on her arm. Why didn't they tell me?" Blondie looked puzzled.

Sam shook his almost bald head, "Yeah, they did. Her heart exploded one day when she'd gone out. 'Member that?" Blondie shook her head, then started to play with her long, loose braid that hung down her back. It was almost undone.

"Mama had chickens. She used to feed them out back. When she'd try to get them off the steps, she'd shoo them with her hand, and they'd flutter every direction. Then she'd flap her apron at 'em. Always wore an apron since she didn't want flour on her flowery dress. All the time she'd wear a flowery dress." Pacing back and forth, Blondie didn't seem to know which way to go. She'd walk a few steps, turn, then go back.

Finally, facing Sam, she stopped, "You're mean!" She shouted.

Turned again, hugging herself, to walk away, still hugging her mid-section.

"Where're you going?" Sam called behind her.

"Don't fret yourself! You got things to do." She said as she reached the corner, muttering. Tears started again. Talking to herself she muttered, "Mama's dead. Why didn't they tell me?" Over and over she said, "Mama's dead.", she turned a corner and was out of sight.

Sam stomped his foot, turned, then went on his way shaking his head, his hands stuffed in his pockets.

"Blondie," She said. "They don't even know my name!" She looked around, tried to see if anyone else was around. "Huh!" Her bitten or bruised lip hurt when she put her fingers on it. "Oh, that hurt." She pulled her bottom lip down, then wiped her finger on the plaid shirttail. No one else was close by. Confused, she didn't know where she was.

"Oh, wait, I used to go to the library someplace around here. Maybe it's this way." Walking, staring at strange buildings, she wiped her nose on the long shirt. She kept walking, looking through dark windows, but kept looking around as if afraid someone might be following her.

Cars went past in both directions. None slowed. At a corner, she stopped, not knowing which way to go, she held one hand against a brownstone.

CHAPTER 3

BARRY

A woman and man hurried across the intersection. She jumped, startled, when a voice close by said, "Thank you, sir,"

Holding onto the building, she peeked around the corner. At first, she didn't see anything, then she looked down. Her bruised mouth fell open and she put her right hand over it to muffle any sound.

Leaning back against the building, a deep breath helped her steady herself along with a head shake to wipe out what she thought was an image she didn't want to see.

While the building held her up, another person hurried past, barely slowing down.

"Thank you, ma'am. The voice around the corner said again.

Around the corner, Blondie returned. "Oh, my! It's not in my head." She looked down.

"Hello." Said the man wrapped in a camouflage jacket, a hat with coined in it was on the ground beside him. "Who are you?" He looked up at her.

"I never saw a person without any legs before." Blondie stammered. "How do you get around?"

With a fetching smile, he pulled back the old jacket to uncover part a pallet covered in scraps of rug with wheels underneath. A battered cane rested behind him. "This way." he said.

Reaching behind him, the cane appeared in his ungloved hand. The other hand closed around the hat with the coins. He stuffed them in a pocket and scooted around to face her.

"You are quick!" Her fears gone, Blondie smiled and stared. "You were a soldier?" She asked.

Busy taking the cap and coins out, he pulled the dark blue cap over his head and looked up. "First a land lubber then a Seal", he mumbled. "Sharks got at me. So, here I am. Who are you? Got a name?" He slid back against his side of the building and waited.

She looked around. Pulled her big shirt tighter. After a while she whipped loud enough for him to hear, "They call me Blondie," Hurrying on, she talked a little louder, "But I got a real name. Mama used to call me... uhm,"

She patted the front of her forehead with a palm then mussed the short front of her hair, making it worse than it was, "Mama was big. I was littler. She kept chickens."

The man waited. "You're pretty under that beat up face. You had anything to eat lately?"

She stopped, stared, then laughed. "Eat? Yeah. Sam took me. Where's Sam? Sam's gone some place. You got a name? You can't be Sam too." She laughed and shrugged her shoulders.

"Yeah, I'm Barry. This corner's dried up. You said Sam took you someplace to eat. Where'd you go? I'm hungry and getting cold staying in one place. You may want to eat again. You're so little.

Blondie said, "Okay, let's go eat."

"What did you say your name was?"

She thumped her head again and shrugged.

"Well then. Guess I'll call you Blondie."

Blondie skipped and shrugged, then said "Okay".

They left with Barry pushing his wheeled flat in front.

"How do you manage the curbs?" she said to his back.

"Oh, they're not so easy. I just avoid them when I can." Barry pushed with the broken cane and sped along.

"Mama's dead" Blondie muttered. "She's gone, too."

Barry stopped. Turned toward her.

"Too? Who else do you mean?" Blondie hit at her head again.

"Don't know. All of them, I guess. Don't know."

Silence. Barry shook his head then turned around to go on his way.

"There were little kids there, too. Just like here, I'd see them come in and go out. Some looked hungry too. Some were prettied up. Not like those here who become straggly after a few days. They could have been prettied up—the girls—that is – I don't know.

Barry stopped. He turned toward Blondie. He sat on his wheeled-pad and watched her. Finally, he quietly said, "Where were the little kids who came in and out?"

She looked surprised, then said "At the school of course! I taught literature, of course. To big kids, I did, you know, of course!"

"Oh." Barry looked at her, shook his head, squinted his eyes, and turned to go on.

"All those books we read! Remember the stories—some like Alfred Prufrock. He was something else!" She strutted after Barry; shaking her head, looking proud. "We going to eat now?"

At the end of the block he turned.

"Wait!" She called, not seeing him. "Where'd you go? Can't see you," Blondie looked all around, then peeked around the corner, "Oh, there you are!" Shirttails flying behind her, she caught up. He was waiting, "Where are we going to eat?"

A big white box truck with its front wheels on the sidewalk blocked the way. "Oh, hell," Barry muttered, "Gotta go around. That sucks. No driver in sight, oh, well." He shoved his cushioned pallet to the curb, held on behind him then pushed off his almost—cane, trying not to fall off the homemade pallet he sat on.

Blondie stared, then blurted out, "Wow! You did that like a champ!" She stopped. "Amethyst! Mama named me Amethyst—after my birth stone but I liked it when she called me her little Amy. I like Amy. You can call me Amy."

Suddenly shy, Blondie or Amy turned away.

Barry rolled down the street. Over his shoulder, he called, "Come-on Amy! If you help me up that curb, we're going after burgers!"

"Burgers? I don't have any money. Don't they want money? I don't know." Blondie held back, confused. She kept playing with her braid, now almost undone. "How can I get your—whatever it's called—up the curb? I don't know, I don't know," She kept saying.

"It's easy. Just push my back, I'll do the rest. Come on."

Barry tilted the front up onto the curb. Still hesitating, Blondie carefully touched his back then stopped to wipe her hands down her front.

Barry struggled then said, "Push. Push hard. Under my shoulder blades. That's right, push."

Blondie braced her feet then shoved. He was tough, but she pushed; up he went. Right into a brick sided building.

"Oh, my," she said, "Are you okay? I don't know what made me push that hard."

Barry laughed; his wide mouth stretched past the whitest teeth she had ever seen. She laughed too.

"Burgers!" They kept on laughing. She was twirling around. He was holding his side as they laughed.

"Wait, I dropped my hat, can you fetch it? Glad I put the change in my pocket, yeah." He pointed to the cap laying in the street. Still dancing, Blondie got the hat and handed it to Barry.

He put it on his almost shaved head, then said, "Let's be off. There's a burger joint around that corner but you'll have to open the door and then pay. Here's the money."

Picking at the coins she walked past the store that sold burgers. She smelled something good and raised her head with eyes closed, she stopped and murmured, "Mmmm"

Barry called, "Woah! Come back! Come 'ere!" Out of her fascination with a handful of coins, she'd forgotten about the man on a something that could wheel around trucks but couldn't open doors.

Doors were easy for her but then, she was at least two and a half—How much is that she wondered. Anyway, she moved back and opened the heavy door, she held it with one hand and a knee barely covered by a long tear where her knee poked through her grimy jeans, once blue, now faded in places.

Oh well. Everybody wore torn jeans! Wouldn't be allowed to wear these to school, she thought as Barry scooted past. She tried to put the coins in her pocket and spilled some. Too tight.

Barry scooped up the spilled coins and made his way to the counter, "Come on," he said and looked up at her, "We'll have two specials. She'll pay." He told the heavy-set girl behind the counter who looked over at him then at her. "That'll be $1.75" the girl said. "Sit over there, we'll bring it to you. "As soon as Blondie laid the coins on the counter, the girl picked through them then disappeared around back.

Barry wheeled himself to the first table and moved a chair with one hand, he fit with only his head above the tabletop.

"Come on, Amy." Fill those cups with ice and drinks. Push. Let go when the ice is full. Push under the drinks. That's right. Move away when it's full.

He waited. She murmured to repeat what he said.

"Set our drinks on the table then get us two straws, that's good. Now sit at the table with me."

Blondie put the drinks down. Handed him a straw then bent over to whisper as she stared.

"It's so clean! Mama likes clean, she—"

She was interrupted by a young man with a tray, their burgers, fries, and ketchup. He said nothing but held out his trays. After he left, Blondie said, "Maybe he can't talk." Then she grabbed at a wrapped burger and tore into it as though she'd never eaten.

"Mmmm" Was all Barry heard while he munched fries and watched her stuff her mouth.

"Where do you sleep?" he asked when she paused to sip at her straw.

"Sleep. Gotta sleep." She mumbled with a mouth full. She shook her head, "Mama slept in a big bed. Little one slept next to her. Little one gone now, too. Went with somebody—a woman—in a nice suit." She shook her head, "Gone, now." She swallowed. Shook her tangled head. Mumbled, "Don't know."

Barry watched her, as he slowly chewed, then said, "Don't know where they went, or don't know where you sleep?"

She looked up, pausing to shake a curly fry at him then quickly said, "Library. I sleep sometimes—with books. I read lots of books, you know, Dickens. He's good. Had lots of boys. Liked his boys but they stole stuff. Don't like stealing stuff." Bent over to finish fries stuffed in her mouth, she mumbled something Barry couldn't catch.

He reeled back, "We gotta go, now. Put everything in the trash stand near the door. Let's go."

"Go where? Put papers where? Oh, by the door? Do I open door to go? What do I do? Oh, okay. You okay? Which way? Oh, I see. You go, I go, We go. Okay!" Looking around, she managed to put the tray and papers in the tall brown stand and to open the door for Barry to wheel himself out onto the sidewalk. The door slammed behind them. It started her.

"Where we going now?" She waited, left behind the free-wheeling Barry, she hurried to catch up.

"You said you liked books. Let's go to the library. You sleep there, you said, so you must know the way." He hurried on his padded car-rier, pushing with his half-cane and a set of half-covered knuckles, the first knuckles on both hands were bare, Blondie stopped. Looked around, rubbed her stomach. Looked around some more. Patted her head, then ran to catch up.

"Oh, the burger was good! Fried potatoes, why did I not know they were so good! I can open the door, too. Can we go there? Now? Let's go there! Now!"

"No. We can't go there now. We're going to the library. Where is it?

Blondie sat down on the curb. She put her arm across her knee with her head down and cried. Barry swerved around and went back to her. "Don't cry. You'll remember the way," he thought about patting her on the back, but withdrew his outstretched arm.

Through sobs, she managed to say, "You can't get up the big steps on that whirly-m-jig thing."

"Okay, okay. So there are steps. We only have to go to where the steps are. You know where they are?"

Barry tried not to lose his patience.

Blondie lifted her tear-streaked face.

"You don't get it, do you? I don't know from here!" She stood up. "Go away! You don't get it! Take me back to where you sat! I'll find my own way!" She walked past him. He sat still. Dropped his head in defeat then pushed in front of her.

"I think I know... That's a big building with lots of steps! We'll find it. Then I'll go to my place. You can go to yours. Okay?"

She quit wiping her smudged face. "Where do you sleep?"

"Sleep? What's that got to do with anything?" He blurted out

Blondie stomped her foot. Put her dirty, and now messy hands on her skinny hips. "where do you sleep? Don't you know where you sleep? Do you sleep on that pallet of yours? Where? Don't you know?"

"Stubborn but determined." Barry muttered quiet enough so she wouldn't hear him, "Come on!" He hollered. "You coming or not?" He turned and went on his way. She stood still, letting him go.

After about half of a block, she traipsed after him. Half walking, half skipping.

As she walked up the tall steps and opened the door, Barry scooted away.

"Wait." She called. He kept going.

"Oh, well." She paused and went inside.

"So much for that!" She said as she waved at the lady behind the counter. "Dried up old prune." She muttered to herself, her head held high.

The woman behind the counter watched her without changing her expression.

Blondie kept mumbling Amy, Amy, Amy. That's a good name. "Amy, Amy, Amy. Gotta be Amy, Barry- that must be his name- had no legs below his knees. Called me Amy. Yessirree, a good name, Amy.

She rode the elevator to the second floor where stacks belongs. Without looking around she went forward until she came to a window bolted in by tall bookcases against the window wall. Without looking left or right, she managed to rifle fingers across all the book spines on her way. Near the end, she pulled out a heavy volume by Thomas Wolfe, sat under the window with her back to the wall and hugged the thick volume.

With eyes closed and head slung back, a grin grew across the undamaged sides of her mouth.

After dark, the strait-laced woman found her, still clutching the book, slumped over against the wall. Sound asleep. The woman shook her head, gave a tsk-tsk and left.

The woman returned with a light blanket and pillow. Without disturbing the bruised and sleeping one in an over-sized shirt, the pillow was quickly tucked under her still head. The blanket, still doubled, covered the small being.

Shaking her head, the librarian left. She put a sign indicating "Closed." Was put at the far end of the stacks, to be removed when morning came. Little Amy slept; Thomas Wolfe stayed close.

CHAPTER 4

DARCY

She flew down the steps, turned, went up again, "May I use the bathroom please?"

Another, younger girl was at the front desk on a computer. Without looking up she nodded, raised one hand and pointed around the corner, then went back to her computer without a glance.

As blondie came out of the stall, a tall black woman was at a sink. "My, you're a mess. Do you need me to re-braid your hair? By the way, my name is Darcy. I can wash your T-shirt if you'll take it off."

Darcy kept fixing her own hair and putting on makeup as she talked.

Blondie stood transfixed. "How old are you, little one?" Darcy asked, "you've gotta be more than ten?" Darcy laughed her white teeth gleamed.

"Oh, come on, you can tell me."

Blondie stared at the tall woman with bleached streaks down the front of her shiny dark hair.

"I—I'm... I may be... I..."

Darcy put everything back in her purse, and turned to Blondie, then said "I'll tell you what. Let's go to my place and have some breakfast, okay? You like pancakes, don't you? Well then, it's settled. Let's go."

Darcy turned, and reached out to Blondies arm with a paper towel. She ran some water on it then handed it to Blondie.

"Here. Wash your face. It'll wake you up. There, that's good. Here's another for your hands. I'll just fix your braid a bit, there now. You feel better and surely look better. After your clothes get cleaner, you'll be just fine. Let's go." Darcy pulled out a coat she'd hung over a tall door.

Blondie stared at her face. She had never seen an all-black and white person before. Even the long fingernails were black and white. The dress she wore was white with a black trim, matching her black hair with the white streak that was now tied in a bun. Held in place with long white pins stuck through. Black and white low-heels.

Pancakes! Blondie thought. Mama used to make pancakes. "Oh my," She muttered, "Pancakes!"

Darcy led her out.

Darcy laid a book on the front counter when they left, waved a hand, and said, "I don't need this right now, thanks anyway."

Darcy tripped down the many steps, holding Blondie's arm when she hesitated, confused.

They got in a white car, parked nearby. All leather inside, it smelled good. Blondie sat right. Riding in a car made memories swell. Looking at buildings fly past, she finally said, "I used to drive to school."

"School?" Darcy said. "Did you work there?"

Hesitating, Blondie slapped her forehead a while.

"I taught literature. Before—" She stopped.

Darcy kept driving, then turned onto a quiet street and parked. "Before?" she asked. They waited. Blondie ran her hand through the top of her straggly hair. "They took something out of..."

"She stopped to open the door. "Gotta go." She blurted.

"Wait!" called Darcy, "Don't you want pancakes?" Blondie stopped. Turned to her left then to her right.

"Mama made pancakes" she said to herself. "You make pancakes? Good. Pancakes are good."

Darcy came around the car to catch Blondie by the arm, "Let's go have some pancakes and I'll wash your shirt while they cook."

Blondie went with her, mumbling, "pancakes are good..."

Once inside the small, spotless apartment, Blondie went around slowly, almost but not quite touching each chair, lamp, table with things on the top, everything. All the time mouthing sounds silently.

Darcy shed her lightweight coat, slung it over a coatrack by the door and went behind Blondie. In the kitchen, she called, "Make yourself at home. Take of your t-shirt and I'll wash it while the pancakes cook."

Blondie stopped. She hunched her shoulders, then wrapped the long shirt closer around herself.

She shook her head over and over while she paced back and forth. When Darcy came out of the kitchen with a long wooden spoon in one hand, Blondie retreated to a corner, her head shaking back and forth.

With the spoon behind her, Darcy said, "What's the matter? Don't you want pancakes?" The silent Blondie kept hugging herself and shaking her head.

"Oh, I get it, you don't want to take off your shirt. I won't bite. Go ahead, your boobs don't bother me. I've seen lots of boobs," Darcy laughed, "Bet you've got blonde fur down there, too. We'll play that game after we eat." She went back to the kitchen, still laughing.

"Come and get it." Darcy called.

"No, no, no," she kept saying to herself as she ran down the steps, pausing only enough to look in both directions, she ran, still mouthing no. Not knowing or caring where she was, an intersection with cars stopped, or swerving, she ran through and past all of them. Horns blew, people shouted, she didn't care. She ran until she was out of breath and Darcy's white car was out of sight. Gasping, she leaned against a building. Hands on her thighs, she slid slowly down until her head rested on her shaky arm.

Something rolled, then bumped against her. A little girl hung out the window of a pausing car and said something Blonide couldn't understand. Next to her lay a big round orange. "Musta come from that little girl," she waved picked up the orange and started peeling.

She sat, juice running down her chin. After a while, Blondie rested with her head back on the brick, Grinned, and said to herself, "Ha!

She didn't wear a flowery apron like mama did. Wanted to play with my boobs, she did!" Looked down her front, leaned back again, "thought I must be real young, not to know what she was about." Rested some more, "I'm old. Must be twenty-nine by now. Maybe even thirty, don't know. Mama's gone. But I remember those stories. Tale of Two Cities. I 'member that one. Don't know what cities they are. Wonder what city this is." With half the orange in her hand, she got up to look around. With half the orange in her hand, she got up to look around. Started eating, walking, wiping juice off her chin.

CHAPTER 5

WILLIE

Blondie walked and walked. Stepped over and past two or three bundles laying on the sidewalk. "Guess they're out of it." She said to herself, "Don't know how they can sleep all day, must be up all night. At least they got feet! Ha! Wonder where Barry—is that his name? He must sleep someplace. Maybe the library is someplace." She kept walking, pausing only to shake her head and look around.

Finally, she gave up to sit again near a corner where she could see both directions and watched the cars. She didn't see the fellow who almost stumbled over her outstretched legs.

A short, round man with long dirty brown hair said, "Woah! Almost made me lose my ice-cream outta the cone. Don't you know better than to hide with your skinny legs stretched out like that?"

Blondie stood up fast. "Wasn't hiding!" she answered, eying the remnants of his ice cream, most of it pushed down in the cone.

"Chocolate?" She asked.

"No, Rocky Road. I know you, you're the one those boys went after. I hid. They wanted some..." he handed her what was left of his ice cream, "Sorry about that... I coulda helped. Sorry," Shuffled feet a bowed head with the awkward apology.

Blondie held the cone, not knowing what to do. With melted chocolate running out the bottom, she sucked the end. Took a bite, "Mmm, good."

"They hurt you?" he said, wanting her forgiveness.

Between bites, she shook her head, the braid fully loose now. She ran her fingers through her hair and shook her head some more.

"Sam... Where is Sam? What's your name? You aren't Sam." With a big bite, the ice cream cone was gone. Her hands wiped her front,

"Do you have a name? That was good! I'd say thank you, but I don't know your name." She started walking away.

"Will, or, William, Willie." He stammered. She turned. Crossed her arms, shook her head.

"Don't you even know your own name? So which is it, Will or William, Willie? That's funny, three names all together." Laughing as she put all his names together, "Oh, boy. Don't want to call you all three!" Laughing again, she turned once more to leave.

"Wait, I don't know your name either. Just call me Willie." He scuffed a toe and looked down, shy, while he looked at her through his thick eyelashes.

She turned and said, "You can call me…" She used the palm of her hand to pat her forehead. After three or four pats, she said "Amy! You can call me Amy! Mama called me Amy, so there!" She hugged herself. Proud, she stood taller.

With more confidence, he said, "Where you off to, Amy?"

"Off to? What's that? I'm not 'off' to read books!" She walked away. He followed.

Suddenly, she jumped, pointed, and hollered, "There it is! Oh, my! There it is! I can see them from here!"

"What? What are you so excited about?"

"Don't you see? That tall cream-colored building! Looks like its about to fall over! It better not, I got there. Read books, I taught literature, don't you know."

Silence followed. "I'm not a crow." She said.

Will was busy unbuttoning his sweater. He had buttoned it crooked but stopped when he heard her say 'crow'.

"Crow. What's a crow got to do with anything?" he asked, "What do you see? What are you talking about?"

She sat down on the curb, pulled out a foot and kicked it at a wildly painted scooter next to the curb.

"Woah! Don't do that." He caught the scooter before it fell but it had lost one of the helmets left loose on the handlebars.

"Why not! I'm tired of walking!"

He moved the scooter a bit and put a helmet on his head. He bounced the other helmet from one hand to the other.

"So, ride. You can ride, I guess."

"Ride what? Ride what? Ride what?" She asked, "I used to have a car, but won't ride those taxis that pick up just anybody. Besides, they cost. Don't have any money. Usta have some coins from Sam, where's Sam?" Despondent again, she sat still with her first under her chin.

He straddled the scooter, kick started it, and said, "Come on, get behind me. Lets go, I think I know how to get there."

The noise of the scooter startled her. She jumped up; eyes wide. "Get... You think... Oh, dear. You think... Oh, dear..." She stammered. Her eyes squinted. She slapped her forehead, paused, then smiled. She hopped on as if she'd ridden dozens of times and gone so many miles. Reaching around him she grabbed the helmed he'd put over his shoulder, stuffed it onto her head and said, "Lets go! Whee! Lets go!"

In and out in-between the cars, they went. She buried her face against his back and held onto him for dear life, eyes closed, her hair flying every which way.

"Oops", she heard as the motor sputtered. He stopped. With just enough room between parked cars to slip the scooter next to a curb. She raised her head.

"What happened?" She asked.

"Guess it was further than I thought. Forgot to get gas. Guess we'll push a while." He said sheepishly.

"Push? Push what?" Still sitting on the funky scooter, she started smoothing down her hair. She gathered most of it over where she could begin to braid behind one ear.

Willie stood with both hands on his hips and shook his head. The helmet was on the scooter, letting him scowl before he looked one way then another down the street.

"Don't see one," he said.

"One what?" Blondie looked around for something to tie the end of her braid, holding the end of it.

Off the bike, she went over to Willie and handed him the end of her braid. "Hold this," she said.

Before he could do anything else, she stuffed the end of her braid in his hand and turned to tear off the end of the big shirt. Willie's mouth was open, but he stood still while she tore.

"There, now. Gives me some color. You like it?" She whirled around. Willie scratched his head.

He then tied down the scooter with a lock cord that he threaded through fastened straps on both helmets, drew out a folded cover from his satchel to spread over the scooter, grabbed Blondie by the arm and started walking.

"We won't push. I'll just hope that they have a little gas can. Lets go! "He said as he pulled Blondie along after him.

"Where are we going? Where are we?" She managed as she tried skipping to keep up, she was dragged along behind him. Willie was quiet, looking both direction from an intersection. She finally looked both ways with him...

"What are we looking for?"

"A gas station, you ninny... see one?"

"With a Pegasus? I read books, you know." Looking both ways, she tugged at her braid, patted her forehead, pulled her arm away from him, rubbed her arm, then hollered. "Wait! I see one! There's a flying horse! Didn't know horses could fly." She stopped to stare with one hand shading her eyes.

"It's only a few blocks, come on!" he grabbed her arm to speed them up. She almost fell off the curb. He pulled and hurried across the intersection, holding out a free hand to halt traffic. People hollered, blew horns. They went as fast as his short legs in the loud pants could move.

At the service station, he asked a man who was washing a car with a long hose if they had a gas can. The man dropped the hose, water still running across the pavement. He nodded to Will, "This way," was all he said, and walked inside a bay.

Blondie stared at the running water. She picked up the hose and doused herself, giggled, then shivered as the cold water hit her shirt. Splashed her face. Giggled some more. Wiped her face with the ragged shirt tail.

Willie, followed by the man, had a red, empty gas can in his hand. Both stopped to watch blondie with the t-shirt plastered to her front. Giggling, Blondie waved the running hose at them. "Whee!" She shouted and waved.

They looked at each other. Both ran toward her, but she saw them, laughed, crouched, sprayed water at them, then ran and laughed some more.

Two against a laughing water sprite. The chasing, spraying, laughing went out of Blondie. Suddenly, she stopped, threw the hose away. Sat down. Dropped her head onto her hands and cried. Her shoulders shook.

The two men look at her then at each other. Dripping wet, they slowly went to her. Neither was sure what to do. Wiped water off themselves. Waited.

The garage man suddenly remembered the water hose and went to turn it off. Willie looked at the red gas can and went to fill it half-way full, glancing at Blondie every few seconds. She stopped crying and sat still where she was. Willie stopped filling the can when he saw Blondie carefully get up. She brushed away tears and dried her hands on the front of her long shirt but stood still.

The garage man came out of the bay but kept his distance. Willie went to him, held out his free hand to thank him,

"How much?"

"Oh, I don't know. Maybe a couple bucks. She gonna be okay?"

"Guess so," Willie sighed. "Don't know. Thanks, anyway."

Willie dug a couple of dollars from his pocked and gave them to her helpful stranger.

Willie led Blondie away, still holding her shirt sleeve. She looked back at the garage man. Waved as best as she could, then went along with the tongues of her sneakers sticking out.

"Tongues" she said, "why'd anyone call them 'tongues'?" she kicked one up to better see the tongue.

Willie didn't answer. Clinched his jaw and kept walking, holding Blondie's sleeve.

After twists and turns, they finally saw the scooter. Somebody—or the wind—had thrown the cover against a building some feet away.

"Damn!" came out of Willie's mouth. He let go of Blondie's sleeve and the gas can in order to chase after the billowing cover.

The cover wasn't big, but it half covered him. He came back to find Blondie already sitting on the scooter, re-braiding her pigtail, the ragged tie draped across one thigh. She tied it around her pigtail and smiled at Will.

Folding the scooter cover small enough to fit in a box on the side of the scooter, he said nothing but looked disgusted.

"Where we going now?" She grinned.

"Humph. To that tall building, I guess." He said as he poured gas into the scooter's tank. "That is, if you still want to."

"What tall building. I don't see any tall building." She was brushing her t-shirt that had dried but was cleaner than she was. She picked at her front, trying to scrap off the remnants of blood.

He climbed aboard, saying nothing. Looking backward, he gingerly backed away from the parked cars, stopped long enough to be sure he was clear and said, "Come on, get on. We're going now." And shot forward.

Blondie was slung backward, but quickly grabbed him around his thick middle.

"Woah... Whee!" She muttered before her face and head were buried behind him. Hand that helmet back," she hollered, "I'm blowing away!"

With one hand, he unfastened the spare helmet and handed it back to her. "Maybe it's good that you blow away!" she didn't hear what he had mumbled while he pushed his own helmet onto his bent-over head.

Whizzing between and around traffic, they stopped in front of steep steps. He took off the helmet. She looked up, took off her helmet, shook her head.

"Where... oh, the steps. I remember the steps." Off she came, "We're at my library, yes?" She gave him the helmet, looked at him.

"Are you going away, too?" she asked.

Willie sat still.

"Sam went away. Don't know where Sam went."

Whizzing up the steep, broad steps, she stopped near the top and looked back. Willie was going around a corner.

"Oh well." She said as she went up the rest of the steps and opened the tall door.

CHAPTER 6

PLAIN ED

The same young girl behind the desk was buried in a book and didn't look up. Blondie headed toward the bathroom. She put her hand on the door pull. Slapped her head with the palm of her outstretched fingers and palm. Stood still, slapped her head again. Turned loose, stepped backwards and left with the door still closed.

Shaking her head, she went out the front door and down the steps slowly. She sat at the bottom, her head in both her hands.

Covered in a heavy comforter with only a shaved head covered in cap, someone trudged past. Blondie heard the covering slide past. She looked up, the person—she thought it was a man—looked at a small phone, maybe. It trudged on. She shook her head and looked down again.

She wished she had a phone. Had heard rumors, didn't know where she'd put it. Turned the page of an imaginary book, dialed an imaginary telephone, one of the old kinds that went round and round. Got up, said "Burgers, mm". Walked, not knowing where.

With her head down, Blondie didn't notice that the sky had darkened. Wind had picked up. Muttering to herself, she tugged the long shirt tighter around her and put her hands under her arms. The wind blew stronger, she kept walking and talking to herself. Dodging some folks with umbrellas, she began to notice a few raindrops.

She stopped, held out her hands to catch a few droplets. Suddenly, skies grew black, rain fell harder. Not noticing where she was, she backed into a doorway. It was unlocked, she fell through the door.

"Oh my! That was hard!" She said out loud.

"What have I done?" She murmured.

Then she saw him. There was a man, standing against the wall of a long hallway. Stairs that went somewhere went up to his right.

"Well, hello." He said as she scrambled up. "Come on in, else you'll get wet." He laughed.

He took one look at her and decided she was not used to scrambling from the rain and wasn't quite sure how to handle surprises. She stared and hit her head with her palm.

"Don't be afraid, I wanted to get out of the rain, so I came in here." He said. She stared, fidgeted with the sleeves of her shirt, then turned her back to him and patted her head over and over.

There were mailboxes along one wall, she quit bouncing her palm on her head to walk along the boxes. Each one had a different name on it. Pointing a finger, she traced the name on each one, going closer to him each step. Suddenly, she stood as tall as she could, next to the man."

"Do you have a name?" She asked, defiant.

"Well, yes." He answered.

"You're white!" she blurted

"No, I'm Edward Thomas Fields," he said, grinning. "Some call me Eddie. Others call me plain Ed, a few call me Mr. Fields. What's your name?"

"You have too many names! There's no name like yours on these!" She laid her hand on the box panel, then turned her back to him and walked to the half-opened door.

"It's still raining!" She turned toward him, "You're not wet!" she said, shivered, and pulled her shirt close.

"You're cold, to say little about wet." He took off the long tan topcoat and wrapped it over her shoulders, "There. Better?"

She pulled the braid out and squeezed water from it. The coat smelled good.

"Plain Ed." She stopped, looked up at him. "Can I call you Plain Ed?"

He laughed, got serious and said, "If you want to, I'll be Plain Ed for you. Are you hungry?"

Blondie grinned. "Sam and I had burgers and French fries! Sam's gone." She licked her lips the frowned. A smile lit up her face, "Mmm."

"Well, tell you what. When the rain stops, we will find some burgers, okay?"

"Burgers! Yumm!" she nodded. Pulled his coat closer, turned and went to the half-opened door to peak out. Almost lost the strong-smelling coat as she looked up at the slowing rain.

He dashed to re-cover her shoulders. Their hands met. She looked down at his hands and blushed.

"Oh, no." She threw away the coat—and his hands—to go outside.

Startled, he caught the coat and looked outside.

"See—nothing," she said and turned to him. "Let's go!" She skipped, danced, and twirled with her hands held out, palms up.

He shook his head, grinned, and threw his overcoat over his shoulder to go in front of her.

After several blocks, they turned a corner to find several big bundles with feet sticking out. "Willie was his name—no it was Barry—he had no feet!" she patted her forehead. "He went round and round. Sat on something with wheels. Went everywhere there was a way to go, couldn't go off curbs. They were too bumpy. Went around curbs."

Carefully, she stepped past the bundles. "Zoned out." She murmured. "They must be zoned out to sleep like that. Some are wet from the rain."

She ran to catch up. "I'm not wet anymore," He walked up the edge of the sidewalk not to get too close to the bundled homeless.

She walked backward away from the bundles and chewed a forefinger on the other side of the scabbed over lip split.

The sun came out, Blondie looked up, and danced around, occasionally looking at him, she pushed up one of her sleeves to compare it to his white face. He smiled but kept walking.

They walked along a high chain fence. "That's where all the veterans go." She said and got quiet. She walked beside him. "I don't like that place," she said quietly.

"Why?" he asked, "Do you know someone who has been there?"

"No, they hide in the bushes. Sometimes I see them." She silently reached for his hand.

"Oh, you've got a watch." She lifted his blue shirt sleeve. "Can I see it?"

"My watch? Can you tell time?"

"Of course, silly! My daddy taught me how to tell time by the time I was five years old! Everybody knows how to tell time! She turned loose of his shirt sleeve and ran.

"Wait, tell me more about your dad. Wait!" She stopped. Turned to look at him, walking backwards, "He's gone too. Don't know where he is. Gone, too."

She shrugged her shoulders and waited. "Mama... Mama's gone now She usta have a big picture of him. If he was in a war, does that mean he was a veteran? I don't like this place." She hurried on,

"It was in a big frame," held her arms above her head to make an oval.

"Mama dodged a hammer when he tried to hit her. Broke the picture. Threw it away. I guess... Can we eat soon, now? Mama wore an apron, you know."

Past the VA hospital with it's many buildings, they stopped at a red light and turned the corner as Ed's phone in his pocket rang. He dug it out, looked at the screen, and answered, "Hi, Thomas, what's going on?" He kept walking.

Blondie stopped and stood with her mouth open. She caught up to tug at his sleeve again.

"You got a watch and your... pants ring or twitter or something. Who're you talking to?"

Ed put one hand over his phone to pat her shoulder. He said into the phone, "Just a minute Thomas," and kept walking, taking her with him, "It's okay, let me finish please." There was the smile again.

With her head down, she shook both her hands but kept quiet as she walked and patted her head, murmuring to herself and pulling her shirt closer around her.

"Now, Thomas. Where were we? Oh, nothing. I was talking to a wayward child," he laughed, "No, she's not a child, just a little 'off'" he laughed again. "Yeah, okay, go get 'em cowboy. Talk to you later." He put his phone back into his pocket, looked around for Blondie, she was half a block ahead, walking fast.

"Hey, you." He started to run after her but stopped,

"This way! Come on! We go this way! Where are you going? This way!" He called with both hands cupping his mouth, "Where are you going? Come this way!"

She stopped. Looked around. Slowly, with her head down she stuffed both hands into her tattered jeans. Lost one shoe, turned, picked up her shoe and came toward him with her lost shoe in a hand, hobbling slowly. She tried to say something as she pointed her shoe at him, nothing came out but mumbles. She stopped to put her shoe back on after she slapped it against her leg. Looked inside the shoe to get out a small pebble, or something.

He waited, then waved one arm to get her to come.

She stopped, hopped her shoe on and looked around. Finally, she walked toward him. "I can read you know. My Mama taught me... don't know if I had a brother... he musta gone, too. Batman. He brought me Batman. He coulda been a brother . . . or maybe just a neighbor. I learned to read all the comic books! I know how to read, you know." She patted her forehead again and again.

She stood still and stopped patting her head while she stared at him.

"You know how to read? Anybody with a pocket that jingles and wears a watch must know how to read,"

"Let's go get those burgers." Watching traffic carefully, he took her sleeve-covered hand and crossed the busy street. He was holding holding her shirt sleeve across her hand. She looked at the empty cuff hanging down and giggled.

"You made magic! See—my hand is gone, but I'm still holding on. You have a jingle in your pocket again. That's magic, you know."

As soon as they crossed the street, he let go to take his phone out of his pocket. She kept waiting all the while flapping the cuff that hung from her arm.

"My hand is gone, too, but it's still there!! Ha ha!"

"What?" he said into the phone, "Oh, Christ! Can't you get the part anywhere? Where did you search for it? No, I can't do anything about that right now! Gotta go. Keep looking!"

Blondie kept on walking. She was halfway down the block. He stuffed the phone back in his pocket as he hurried to catch up.

"See? Your magic works! I once knew someone else who made magic. They—he—pulled a thing out of my head—don't know what, but it didn't hurt. Slept a long time after that," She patted the top of her head this time. "Slept a long time."

He shook his head, looked down at her, and gingerly put his arm around her small, slender shoulders.

He had never known anyone as pretty or as helpless as she was, but he didn't know what to do with a memory that was so messed up. He didn't know where she lived or stayed or anything. He just shook his head and looked down at her.

"You still want those burgers?"

"Burgers! Sam—wait, Sam?—or Will on his wheels—Wheel rhymes with Will—Can you... of course you can. You're tall like Sam. Sam's gone,"

He stopped to open a door, "We're here," he said, touching her back so she would go inside. She went in but stayed at the door to look around.

"This is a fancy place." She stood tall and kept looking, "There's a TV!" She stared, turned the other way, "There's another TV. Usta have a TV. I taught school, you know. Usta have a TV but don't know where it went." Giggled and put a hand over her mouth, "TV can't go anywhere. Mama's gone somewhere. She died, you know. This a place to eat? I smell something." She stood closer to him, afraid.

A tall woman came toward them, looked at her, frowned, but saw him and then said, "Right this way, sir."

He put his hand on Blondie's back and whispered, "Follow her," they wound their way past tables. Blondie stared at each person as they went past. He had to keep her going, but she still turned to see what they were eating as she passed, sometimes she turned all the way around.

They sat at the table indicated by the tall woman.

"Jewel will be taking care of you today, if you need anything else, just let her know," The tall woman said as she put menus on the table then walked away.

Blondie leaned over to watch her as she went back to the front then wriggled in her chair as she played with her rolled napkin, "Oh, there's something in here!"

"Yes, unwrap your silverware if you want to," he said.

Jewel appeared. His phone rang again. He turned it off and laid it on the table.

"Just bring her milk, I'll have a dry martini. Also, bring us two waters with lemon. Thanks."

Jewel nodded and left. Blondie watched her go.

"Where'd she go? To get the cow? They got cows in here—else where'd she get milk? Her dress is too short. Why'd she wear black stockings? She's not black." "Shush, please. Not so loud. Just look at the TV, okay?" He patted her arm and wiped his face.

Chastised, she tilted her head to see the TV hung flush with a wall.

Jewel brought her milk and water. His drink was in a a funny long stem glass. There was part of a lemon peel in it. She shook her head. "Why'd they...."

"Are you ready to order?" Jewel interrupted.

"Sure, bring us two steaks, both with fully loaded baked potatoes."

Blondie pointed, "What's a co-vid? There's something in that paper about a co-vid. Lots of folks have something called" co-vid. Is that a car? What's a co-vid?" she asked, fiddling with her hair.

Jewel left. Writing in her little book, she shook her head as she wound through the patrons.

"No, Covid-19 is not a car. It's a virus—a disease. Anybody can catch it."

"I don't do numbers anymore. Can you catch it like fireflies? Put some in a bottle once. They light up like magic. You're magic."

 He shushed her and reminded her to speak quietly many times in between pointing to the televisions so she would remember to watch instead of talking too loudly.

Finally, the food came.

"What's that?" she asked, staring at the big steak.

"It's all red inside," she shoved the plate away but watched him take a bite.

"You don't like it?" he asked

"This is too red."

"Oh, it's not cooked enough," he raised his hand.

"Don't they make burgers here?" she blurted just as Jewel came to the table. She brushed her hair back, "I'll just have a burger please," she said as she shrank into herself without looking at anyone.

He nodded at Jewel. She took away the plate.

"There! I needed that." He said as he pushed away his plate.

"Now, where is my happy girl?" he asked, leaning and smiling across the table. She lifted her chin, trying to look royal, glanced at the television, frowned.

She shook her head, "Why does the man keep saying so many are dead? I don't like dead. Don't like red—looks like blood." She shivered and waiting while he finished chewing. He raised his hand again, and Jewel appeared.

"Make that to go, please."

She left, shaking her head. They sat, not talking. When Jewel came back, she had a white bag in one hand and a brown folder in the other. He took a thick billfold out, gave her a fifty-dollar bill, got up and said, "keep the change,"

Blondie's eyes stared wide. Her hand flew to her mouth.

"Let's go," the bag was still on the table.

"Take your bag, let's go!"

She tumbled out, knocked over the chair, grabbed the bag, and followed him. He turned back to grab his phone.

He walked fast, then turned the corner and waited. At the end of the block away from the restaurant, she slid down the side of the building next to him to scramble through the bag. She pulled out the wrapped burger and spilled fries on the sidewalk. She picked up the fries and stuffed her mouth. "Mmm," she murmured.

She looked up at him looking at her, "What?" she asked with her cheeks puffed out like a squirrel.

He laughed but said nothing.

"Gave her too much. You must have lots,"

"Maybe... Where are you going to sleep tonight?"

"Sleep? It's not dark out yet. Hafta be dark to sleep."

Unconcerned, she shrugged her shoulders and looked in the bag again, then shook it. Folded neatly, she got up and carefully put the bag into a pocket of her jeans.

He pondered a while then said to himself, "A full grown woman with the mind of an eight-year-old." Pondered more then finally said, "So, where will you sleep tonight—after it gets dark?"

Still sitting against the building, she shrugged her shoulders. Shook her head. Put her chin on two fists, tucked her knees up.

"Mama said, 'If it's broken, throw it away.' Who cares?" she paused, then said, "I'm broken. Who cares..."

After a long silence, she looked up, "You gotta go someplace? You going away now? Mama went away. Don't know where she went. Mama woulda kept me, but she didn't have any place. She could draw anything! She would draw pictures when she wasn't stirring that ol' pot with her flowery apron on or when she wasn't calling out docey-does at square dancing."

Blondie stretched out her legs and wiggled her toes.

"Couldn't ever figure out why they called it square dancing. Everybody went in circles. Sometimes she'd play with that ol' organ with the busted keys, she played and played. Had no time for me—since I slept so long—nobody else did neither—oops—sorry, should say 'either'. I read; you know." She stood.

He stood, shaking his head, "Yeah, I have to go now. I have to be someplace." He walked away, shaking his head and rubbing the back of his neck.

"Bye, Plain Ed or Mr. Fields," she said softly, "Sorry I'm broken." She stood still, watching him go. "Wait!" she called. He'd turned a corner and was gone, talking on his magic phone.

"Well. Guess it's about time for me to find somewhere to nestle down. Looks like more rain is gonna come down. She walk-ran to the tallest building.

"Oh, goody! A hotel. Must be somewhere in. Around back, I guess." She stopped. Glanced at the man in front with gold buttons on his navy-blue jacket.

"Must be this way," She back-stepped away, turned the corner and looked for an entrance.

The doorway heavy but unlocked. After going down a few steps, muttered, "Huh. Dark." She held onto a wall, but kept looking, "Oh, good. A light. Back there. Must be back there."

With a big sigh, she saw three big canvas carts.

One was full of sheets and white bundles of damp towels. Next to it, the second big cart was more than she wanted. Her Nose wrinkled from that one. It smelled.

A wall of closed cabinets lined one wall.

"Oh, goody. Bet there's something in there!"

Opening each one, she found folded sheets in one, folded towels in another. She took a sheet and went in head over heels.

Standing up, she spread the sheet over the dirty clothes, wrapped her head and shoulders in the towel and settled into her makeshift bed with a grin, "Warm, cozy, can't ask for better than that,"

Eyes popped open wide. Rolled in the sheet more voices. Several. Too many. Tried to wriggle a foot inside her sneaker but flipped it away. Instead, she left it and snuggled deeper. The voices sounded too close already.

"The first one is full. You can take it to the truck, and it may need both of you. I'll grab the second one. This one smelled too much to leave it there. The last one needs more stuff in it, I'll pitch these things in it, then go to the truck with both of you."

Blondie threw dirty linens away from her head and peeked over the rim to see three hefty women in uniforms go out the door. Scrambling through the linens, looking for her sneaker, she finally held it in one hand and climbed out by the [hardest].

"Oh, my goodness," she mouthed. She hobbled to a corner pulling on her shoe as she went.

She tried to catch her breath behind the jut-out of the tall bricks. As she was about to go out of her hiding place, three women came back through the outside door. They were laughing and chatting away in some language she didn't know.

They went up some stairs, away from Blondie.

"Whooa! That was too close." She said to nobody, as she leaned against the wall. After peaking once more, she ran out the door, a towel still over her head. She pulled it off, as she saw a bright red truck going down the alley.

"Well, at least the rain stopped." She laughed, looked at the towel, and wrapped it back on her head, still giggling,

"Shoulda gone to the bathroom while it was... dear me. Don't know when I'll find another one... Oh, well." She sighed a deep sigh, and kept walking.

"Guess I'll follow that truck best I can. Maybe it'll go to another hotel with a bathroom." She lost sight of the truck.

Wandering, she went past a large building with lots of lights left on. The doors were unlocked. Two sets of doors opened to a wide space that looked like it may have been a basket ball court once, or something.

A woman was busy setting up what look like cots, all different kinds of colors, the woman wore gloves.

"Pardon me, do you have a bathroom? I could sure use a bath-room." Blondie crossed her legs, then held up her fingers, crossed them, and her arms, "Please, ma'am, I could sure use a bathroom."

The woman had on a navy blue, long sleeved shirt with a sewed-on patch over a front pocket that said something about the Salvation Army.

She pointed and kept on putting blankets on the cots.

"There's a shower in there, too. If you need one." She said as she scooted beds away from each other.

Blondie ran the way the woman pointed. She found a sign on the door with a skirt.

"Must not speak English," she muttered. "Oh, well. Doesn't matter" She flew into one of the stalls and quickly threw the towel on the floor.

After flushing, she walked out, pulling at her torn jeans. She looked around.

"Might as well wash up," She giggled. Hopped into a shower clothes and all, and turned on the water. "Brr, that's cold." As she looked close to the knobs, she found H and turned it on too, "That's better!"

Turning to let the water stream down her back, she unwrapped the ragged tie-back and fingered loose her braid.

With her eyes closed, Blondie didn't hear the door open.

"Did you call me?" the woman asked.

"Oh, you scared me!" Blondie quickly turned off the water.

"You sleeping here? Here's some stuff if you are." The woman held a small packet out in a gloved hand.

"You're not sick, are you?" the woman asked.

Blondie looked down at herself, then said, "No. Just wet." She giggled.

"You better go pick out your bed. We fill up as soon as the door opens. Only have 25 beds. Haven't made 'em all up yet, you'll get a blanket and some socks as soon as I get to it," She paused then cocked her head.

Blondie dried as fast as she could. The woman pushed a button at a machine on the wall as she walked out, then stuck her head back in to ask, "How'd you get in anyway? Doors are supposed to be locked until six o'clock. It's not six yet." She looked at the big clock next to the basket-ball hoop.

Blondie shrugged, "Doors were open. So, I came in." She re-plaited her long hair that was still dripping. She walked to a red cot without anything on top. Shook her head and went to a blue one that was against a far wall, but still close to the shower.

"Next time, I'll wash my clothes proper," she said and nodded her head. The woman handed her a blanket and a pair of socks and mumbled something like 'she would help any way she could.'

"Go lock those doors!" the woman clearly said and went back to fixing the cots. She wanted to be sure they were at least a lot of feet apart. Blondie locked the doors.

She went back to the cot she had picked out. Still damp, Blondie wrapped the blanket around herself and sat down like a zombie. She tilted and tugged some more in her sound asleep state. Once she was prone, sleep followed quickly.

Noise woke her up then someone plopped a paper bag onto her cot.

"What? What?" She rubbed her eyes and looked around. People were all over the place. Half-broken carts were pushed up to at least half the cots. People sat or slept on all of them. A girl dropped paper sacks on each cot then left in a hurry.

One young man even had a boom-box that played more static than music. Whatever it was, a man in a uniform of some kind walked over and turned it off. He said something to the littler guy with the now silent boom-box and shook his head. The little guy slammed his fist against his leg then lay down, still mad.

After she pulled the socks up more, Blondie looked around. She didn't see the woman who'd set up the cots. Scrambling inside the bag that was placed so quickly, she found a wrapped biscuit with an egg and sausage inside. She laid them beside her and looked inside the bag again.

"Oh, goodie! An apple. Haven't had an apple for the longest," she exclaimed. "I hafta save it!" She unwrapped the biscuit and took a bite while she hid the apple inside her shirt and the blanket. Still sleepy, she chewed the biscuit and sausage and looked around.

The little man was mad again. He jumped up, grabbed his paper bag, his blanket, and the boom-box and went out! It was still dark outside. (Three new folks wanted to come in.)

"Oh, well. That's tough," She said. "At least he left the cot," She giggled. "How can I leave and go to that bathroom?" She said with her mouth full. The woman came up behind her. She jumped and spun around, the apple falling on the floor.

"Here." The woman said, "take your bag, the blanket, and your toothpaste things I gave you last night. There's a little bar of soap, some shampoo, and other stuff in there. You gotta go, anyway. These cots gotta be ready for the next group. There's already a line outside. Hot meals are for later, next door."

Blondie gathered her things and looked toward the bathroom.

"Go ahead." The woman nodded toward the door on the other side of the room. Blondie, her blanket trailing after her, hurried to the room with the 'skirt' on the door.

"There's a comb in there too, if you decide to use it." Blondie turned her tangled head and kept going.

She came out, looking better than when she went in. Her blanket folded under her arm and her plait straight down her back, the woman was gone. Blondie turned around near the outside doors to look for her again.

As she walked slowly, backwards, she bumped into someone, her things went flying as she almost fell. Hurrying to pick up, she was scrambling after the apple when the man's long legs went over and around her. He kept going.

Stooped, with her apple in one hand and the blanket hunched under one arm, she mused, "Wonder why that fella has that white thing hanging round his neck? A mask is supposed to be black and be put over the eyes if he is to look like the Lone Somebody. Huh! Guess they never read funny books. Oh, well. Must be... something..." She left, trailing her blanket.

People bumped and shoved her, trying to get in. One knocked her over with a cart with one wheel missing. She fell. Laid flat to the walkway, her apple rolled in a gutter.

"You drunk, or what?" one woman yelled toward her.

Blondie's knees were raw from scrambling away. She stood up, shook her head, and ran in the opposite direction. Leaning against another empty building, she stopped to catch her breath, the blanket had to be re-folded and stuffed under her arm. Again.

She smelled something. Not food. She shook her head and looked around. There, there's smoke coming from across three or four streets. She kept walking.

Big and black, coming from the back of that Chinese place! "Must be Chinese, else why is that cross- hatch all across the front?" she mumbled.

She heard sirens but too many cars were zooming past, she climbed onto a red thing by the curb to see better. A big red truck came and stopped. Four men jumped off and ran to undo a long flat hose off the truck. Two of the men stopped next to her and frantically said, "You need to move so we can get to the water. Hurry along; NOW!"

"Water? What? There's no water. Can't..." They pushed her away then unplugged the hydrant she'd stepped up on. Water went everywhere.

Blondie ran back to the building she'd leaned against. People spewed out the front door of the Chinese place across the street. Some of the women had on shiny dresses with big glittery flowers on them. Others wore plain tops with trousers and flat black shoes. One carried a young child who cried and cried, all the time clinging to the one carrying her.

Those red trucks and cars came. People walking made a crowd, but two men kept them back from the hoses. Blondie had never seen such! She gaped and strained to see what was going on... she couldn't for the taller ones in front of her. Frustrated, she managed to duck and twist through the people until she was clear. A block away she could still smell the smoke and see the water plume as it shot from the hoses.

She sat down with her back against a small white structure, "Whew! Don't like that a bit! Too much for me! Musta been... don't know what it musta been..."

Suddenly, she got up and ran. The blanket, under one arm, was partly unfolded and flapped behind her. She held tightly the brown bag and the small black pouch as she ran.

A man was walking across the way, "Might be... Looks like..." she chased him most of the block when he turned and faced her.

"Are you following me?" he asked, "Do you want something?"

She abruptly stopped. Her hand flew to her mouth. She shook her head in confusion but dropped the small black pouch the woman from the Army had given her. She looed up.

He was still standing there, but now his coat was pushed aside and both fists were at his belt. A gun in a holster was next to his pocket.

"Thought you were... someone else... you are... not." Gulping, she backed away, turned and ran as fast as she could.

CHAPTER 7

THE CHILD

Catching her breath, she stopped at the corner where she saw a little girl standing by herself.

"Woah there, what's this?"

No people were in sight. No one else was there. The child was alone in an empty parking lot with a few boarded-up places. Worn out stripes showed where customers once left their cars.

Midsized, next to a curb without any sidewalk, the buildings looked as deserted as the parking lot. The baby girl looked at Blondie but said nothing.

Blondie slowly walked toward the child, "That's what she is, just a child." Blondie said under her breath, "wonder why she's here, by herself." Blondie looked around, saw no one. Not even any cars going past.

Blondie got closer. She sat on her heels then moved so her knees touched the rack-strewn empty lot. She was about the same height as the child but still several spaces away.

The child's dark hair was pushed back away from her streaked face. Tears that had flowed, left their tracks down to a dimpled chin.

Dark eyes, sheltered by thick lashes, closed. When they opened again, Blondie was still there. Still quiet.

The thin dress, with light colored piping on the sleeves showed skinny legs sticking out from a too short and well-worn dress of some kind.

Blondie put her belonging down and held out her hand, "Are you by yourself?"

The child looked at her but said nothing.

"Do you talk?" Blondie asked.

"Do you know English?" Silence.

After a while, Blondie got up, brushed her knees, and gathered her stuff. Her half eaten biscuit spilled out. She brushed it off and took a bite. While munching, she turned to go. She heard a sound and turned back.

"What did you say? Did you say something? I didn't hear, what did you say?"

Pointing to Blondie's crushed paper and the half-eaten sandwich, the child mumbled, "Eat."

Blondie looked at her left-over lunch, then at the child, "Oh, are you hungry? Here, you can have this." She held out her hand with the almost gone biscuit but waited to see if the child moved toward her.

Dirty bare feet came a few steps. Holding out a dirty hand, the child looked at the held-out food then took a few more uncertain steps.

She snatched the food then stuffed it in her mouth, some of it fell. She bent down to pick up the pieces and stuffed them in with the others.

When she stooped to pick up the crumbs, her panties showed. Not only where they grimy, they had holes in them from her scooting around.

Blondie had the empty paper bag in one hand but kept mashing it close to her chin and shaking her head. The child wiped her hands down the front of her dress, looked around, but said nothing.

Blondie sighed. She patted her forehead. Finally, she said, "Well. That's that."

A lone beat-up car went past. Noisy. The man driving it did not turn his head, just kept going. The child held out one arm. Her hand kept opening and closing splayed fingers toward Blondie.

"You want more, huh. No more. See, all gone." Blondie shook the crushed bag. Held it upside down, "See, all gone."

The child shook her head slightly and said, "Gone."

"You do know words! That's... that's good. Do you know your name? What's your name? What can I call you? What's your name?"

The child shook her head slightly, and said, "Gone!"

"Gone... food is gone," said Blondie, "But that's not a name. Do you have a name? What... is... your... name" Blondie spoke slowly.

"Bn" mumbled the little one. She looked at Blondie.

"Ben, huh? That's all? Just Ben? Can't call you Ben. That's z boy's name. Are you a boy? How about I call you Brenda? Is that okay? I'll call you Brenda, okay?"

The frightened child nodded. Took a few steps, then went closer.

"Okay, Brenda. We can go now. Too many folks may come this way. Besides, it's getting darker. We need to find someplace safe. Don't want to be here when it gets dark, Mama..."

Blondie hushed. She folded the blanket again and started to move, "You gonna stay here?" she asked.

With a small shake of her head, she walked to Blondie. Up close, she slipped her grimy hand into Blondie's and looked up at her.

Blondie looked down. Shook her head, and smiled, "Okay... I guess. Lets go."

They walked.

Blondie kept looking for both the leaning top of the library, or the long lines of homeless people waiting for the homeless center. Since she had no idea where they were, she didn't know which way to go.

The child stopped. Turned loose of Blondie's hand and sat down.

"What? Are you tired? Oh, my. You are tired and cold. Here. Wrap in this blanket. We can rest now."

Blondie sat beside her to wrap the child who fell over in sleep. Her head was on Blondie's lap. After looking at the child in her lap, she leaned against the building and sighed. Too confused to sleep, Blondie just sat and leaned. Two people, pushing piles of things in their carts, went past. Neither of the two paid them any attention.

"Wait, where are you going? You going to the center?" She picked up the sleeping child to go after them. They kept walking without even a glance.

"Shh, go back to sleep," She said.

Skinny as she was, the baby girl was heavy. They followed anyway.

After a few blocks, Blondie woke the child to set her down. She wiped the child's dried hands on the tail of the long shirt. It didn't do much good. They both rested a while; still trying to keep the pilgrims with the carts in sight.

The little one was a trooper. She never once complained. Occasionally, she'd whimper. That's all. Blondie sighed again.

The pilgrims turned a corner.

"Gotta go!" Blondie stood and held out a hand.

"Come on. They musta turned or something. Let's go."

Brenda stood, reached for a finger and was awake finally. They hurried to catch up when the pilgrims turned a corner.

"Oh, goodie! I see the big center. It's close. Now I know how to go. Come on, they have food in there!"

Bella looked up, she said, "Food,"

Blondie smiled, "Yes. Food. Lets go eat."

They went on as best as they could. Two broken ones.

Inside, Blondie looked for the Army person. She was near the big doors that led to the kitchen. She spotted Blondie, came forward, looked at the two and stopped.

"What have we here? Where'd you get the young'un?"

"Don't know what to do, looked for food. She's hungry I guess," Quietly, Blondie said and laughed a little, "So am I, I guess."

The woman pondered, turned and said, "Wait here." They waited. No beds were empty except ones by the wall where the pilgrims were beginning to put their meager belongings.

Outside the kitchen doors, the woman talked to Blondie, "A volunteer woman here may be able to help. She's been here for five or six months or so. Comes in early—very dependable. Ties her mostly gray hair in a tight bun and wears a net over it. Wears clean white sneakers and jeans that always look new. Those jeans—never saw anything like it—But she's good at helping the cooks." The Army woman kept looking at the cots to see if one might be empty soon.

"By the way, when you ask her why she cries all the time, she goes to the bathroom and leaves to cry some more, I guess. Oh yeah, brings a big white apron with her to wear. You know, the kind, with a top strap that goes around the neck. Long, it is." She paused. "Never gets it dirty. But the next day, it's like new. Ironed and all. Never seen anything like it!"

The Army woman kept checking spacing the beds. She moved constantly. She checked the separated cots, then looked to make sure they were far apart enough.

She left again and went into the kitchen. "May do some good, I don't know. We'll see. I'll go get her; you stay here." They stayed. Blondie and the child watched. They stayed out of the Army woman's way.

The Amy woman went through a swinging door. Blondie saw her talking with the volunteer. Her hands pointed to the Blondie and Brenda.

At the serving area. The Volunteer and the child looked at each other. Blondie and the child stood in front of the long counter where two men stirred the stews in large pots.

Finally, the child held out both arms and said, "Mama." The Volunteer held her breath, then held her stomach. She went around the long counter than ran toward the child without saying anything.

When she could, she reached toward the child then stopped.

Finally, she said, "Is that you? You've grown so much! You're so dirty. Can that be you? Are you my Brenda? You've been gone so long! Is that my baby? You're so thin."

The child, with her arms still held out, said, "Ben. Mama?"

They both cried. The mother finally hugged the skinny child, "Yes. Oh, yes. You are Brenda!" They walked and hugged.

The volunteer picked up the shy child and went over where Blondie and the woman from the Salvation Army stood waiting and talking

"Can I take her home? She needs a bath. I've still got her clothes." She laughed through the tears that fell off her chin. "Probably won't fit anymore. She's grown so much." Can we go now? I don't plan to be back, will it be... can I call my husband at his work? He won't believe me, but can I call now?"

"Woah! Hafta call the authorities, I guess. You're sure about—" she tilted her head toward the child who clung to the volunteer mother with her head buried, "We gotta call... well, anyway, we can't just... I dunno... Somebody'll know but..."

The Army woman turned and went through the swinging door to the kitchen with her hands scratching her head and waving in the air. She didn't see Blondie trying to say something to her.

Blondie, meanwhile, was looking at a lone cot near the wall without anybody on it. She grabbed the Volunteer by the arm and pulled,

"Come on, there's one over there. Hurry," The

Volunteer with the child looked where she pointed, turned to glance at the kitchen and hurried after Blondie. The child clutching tight and hung on. Her face still buried.

All three went to the empty cot and waited. They sat. Blondie looked around.

"Why do some folks have those white things on their faces?"

"Do you not know about the pandemic the virus has caused?"

Blondie started to say something but movement on the cot stopped her.

The Volunteer had put the child beside her so they would be more comfortable. She hugged as they scooted together.

"Oh, dear. Why is she not clean! She has always been clean. Always smiling. So happy. So full of laughs."

Tears started to form in her eyes as she fidgeted with the straightening the child's dress over thin legs and bare feet.

Blondie grabbed the blanket that had come loose and covered the child's dress and dirty feet so the Volunteer could be calmer. She wound up covering part of the Volunteer, too.

"Eat." Came a sound from Brenda. They both looked at the little bundle.

"Oh, yes." Blondie stood up, "Eat. That's good."

Two policemen came out of the kitchen, followed by the woman with the Army patch on her long-sleeved shirt.

"What's your name?" The burly cop asked. Blondie thumped her forehead with her fist again.

The Army woman said, "She don't know her name. Hasn't told me her name yet. All she does is sleep in wet clothes. Must stay by the creek and keeps falling in. She ain't no part of this. Just found this baby here a place to sit, ain't that right, hun?"

The Army woman kept motioning around her back for Blondie to keep quiet, she failed. Blondie started to explain,

When she said, "I found..." The Army woman put her fingers around her own mouth and went, "Hurumph! Is there anything else, gentlemen?"

She crossed her eyes at Blondie to make her be quiet and tilted her head.

A passerby asked, "Don't you ever listen to the radio?" Blondie kept shaking her head, then said, "I had a radio once, don't know where it went. Musta... Don't know..."

Of the uniformed policemen who came out of the kitchen, one was young and big, the other older and shorter. An older civilian man seems to be with them.

They were protecting him from something, or else he was a detective. The Army woman hadn't had time to call anybody, or for them to get here, Blondie thought. It must be that something else is going on. Blondie sat still. She thumped her hand on her head with her palm and kept sitting.

The three men walked between each row, but finally stopped next to the pilgrims. Blondie's eyes followed. One of the shaggy pilgrims got up to leave.

"You," one of the policemen said, "Stay where you are!" The man moved his cart and kept going through the doors.

The policeman did nothing to stop him. He watched then said, "Oh, well. One less piece of trash."

While their backs were toward Blondie, the Army woman hurried to the front of Blondie's cot, she shushed.

The three policemen turned around. "What's your name?" The one civilian with the two policemen said. Blondie thumped her head with her fingers closed.

"Don't you know your own name?" Blondie thumped her head again. The Salvation Army answered for her.

"No. Else why would she not tell anybody? Please quit asking. She don't know."

After this, the men went from one row to the next, looking hard from one the next, they didn't stop. Finally, they went out without a word.

"Phew..." The Army woman said. "Musta been looking for some-body special. Now I'm gonna try to make that call to my supervisor. He'll know what to do."

She walked to the kitchen. The Volunteer was still petting the head of the child who was still asleep, wrapped in Blondie's blanket. They waited.

The Volunteer wanted to call her husband. Without a phone, she could only stare at the child and wipe muddy grime away from the child's face as best as she could, between wiping away tears that fell from her own face.

Blondie was happy to be sitting down for a change. She had walked as far as she could manage.

One shoe even felt funny. She scooted to the end of the cot and raised one foot across the other knee.

"No wonder!" She said and took off the shoe. She held it up to look through it. She giggled and stuck her hand in the shoe with her forefinger poking through the hole. "My new sock now has a circle of dirt on it!" She paused, then said, "Do you want some socks? The lady gave me socks last... don't 'member when..."

Blondie put her shoe back on and slumped over.

The Volunteer shook her head as if to say "no." She petted the sleeping child and talked nothings to her

The Army woman backed through the kitchen doors, she had blue ceramic bowls on the tray she carefully carried. A biscuit sat on a small plate with three big spoons stuck in the bowls. Two of which were full. The third bowl was mostly broth with a few vegetables in it.

Others on their cots rolled over, mumbled, or sat up, "Go back to sleep!" the Army woman hollered, "This is not for you!" she almost whispered, "Now you can eat something."

Blondie scooted over to make room between the grownups as the tray was set down.

"Here's some stew. The little one's is mainly the soup part. Didn't know how much she'd eat." The Volunteer perked up as the child said, "Eat". The child shook off the mother and spread her arms towards the bowls.

"What about your phone calls?" The Volunteer asked. The Army woman had both hands behind her back.

"Well." She said, "I don't know. I explained as best I could to my supervisor. He listened then went quiet. He said he'd have to talk to some other folks. So, --- I don't know. Guess we'll have to wait for him to call back. I just don't know." She moved her hands from her back, fluttered them, then shrugged her shoulders.

Blondie worked her bowl empty and set it back on the tray. The child had grabbed her own bowl with both hands. She drank and drank. Pieces of potato and carrots were left. She dug them out to stuff them in her mouth.

The Volunteer started to stop her, but she finally left her alone to dig out the remnants. She shook her head and just stared, while her bowl was left untouched.

"Eat" said Brenda, holding out her bowl for more. The mother spooned some broth from her bowl. They both smiled, the child ate, her head buried in the bowl.

A man with a tall white hat stuck his head out of the kitchen. He waved for the Army woman to come, then disappeared.

"Gotta go," the Army woman hurried to the kitchen, leaving the tray and two empty bowls behind.

The two adults looked at each other.

The child wiggled. She shed the blanket and crawled off the cot, held her bottom and said, "Pot, pot."

"Oh my, she has to go to the bathroom" half running, the

Volunteer took the child around the corner into the lady's room. Blondie got half up, then sat down. She smiled as she watched the two hurry to the bathroom.

Not quite rested, Blondie sat and looked around. Some of the people around her were getting up. Others seemed too asleep to move. Others began to form a line, waiting for the bread and stew that was bring brought out. A few had white things hanging around their necks.

"What did she call them? Oh, that's it. Masks." She smiled, "I 'membered–yea!"

Proud of herself, Blondie got up and twirled around. The child was cleaner when they came out of the lady's room. Holding hands, and smiling, both were damp and a bit wet but a lot cleaner.

"I tried to wash her off. She turned the handle on the shower but ran out away from the water. I think it must have scared her. But she liked the warm air from the hand dryer. Oh, well. So we're both drowned rats." She wiped herself, "I'm dirty too, now."

Brenda climbed up and tried to wrap herself up in the blanket. The Volunteer saw what the child needed and fixed it for her. "She's a climber. Been a climber since she was... oh, my." Her hand flew to her mouth. "Her birthday was only last..." Crying, she leaned down to hug the child. Blondie was confused. She bumped her head between both hands then shook her head. She pointed to the young child, "How old?" She asked.

"Three now" The mother said between sighs and wiping off her tears.

The Army woman pushed out of the kitchen. She walked toward the cot slowly with her head down.

"Talk to the supervisor. He's thinking, may call... may not. Don't know. We'll see."

One of the servers came out of the kitchen, spotted the Army woman, and waved for her to come back.

"Gotta go," she said and hurried. Talked a minute or less to the servers, and flew into the kitchen

The Volunteer and Blondie looked at each other and then to the child, who was still rolling the blanket around herself.

The Volunteer helped her, then she fingered the piping on the sleeve. "This used to be white. Picked out this dress myself. We were outside when the phone rang. A wrong number, it was just a second. She was practicing walking, I guess. When I went back out to check on her, she was nowhere! I looked and looked! No matter how much I, plus most of the neighbors looked, we couldn't find her."

Fingered the piping some more, she wrapped the blanket closer.

"Just look at it now! The piping's almost... It's been almost a year. Ten months and fourteen days! I've can't explain how much we looked! I only came here because I was hoping somebody might come in with her." She buried her salt and pepper head in the blanket, wrapped the child and tried not to sob, but she couldn't help herself.

Suddenly, she gathered up the child and stood.

"They've got to let us go home! I need to call my husband!" Blondie, still sitting, helplessly looked at them.

The Army woman came out walking slowly with both hands on her mouth, shaking her head. When she got close enough, she stood still, but kept shaking her head. Finally, she said, "Don't know what to do. Finally got through to my supervisor, he don't know what to do either."

She took a deep breath. "After he made a lot of calls, he never could get anybody but finally gave up. He asked me over and over, was I sure."

She gulped, and went on, "After the longest time, he said he didn't know what to do. Finally, he said if I was sure, let them go, but never—and he meant never—tell anybody." The Army woman leaned against the wall, "So—go!" Standing straighter, the

Volunteer glanced at Blondie, shuffled her weight with the child under the blanket and ran out the front door.

The Army woman glanced at Blondie, moved her weight from one foot to the other and said, "He tried to call, tried and tried. Put his job in danger. Had to make his own decision—nobody to tell him what to do."

She looked at Blondie then sat on the cot with her.

"Guess I'll have to get you another blanket. You stay here." She patted the cot and got up.

Blondie sat still, took off her shoe and lay down, looking at the shoe from all sides, she put her fingers through the hole and giggled. Still holding her shoe, she furled up and fell asleep.

The Army woman came back, shook her head, unfolded the blanket and spread it over Blondie.

"Guess we'll have to keep you in case any of the so-called authorities show up." The army woman walked away with her head down. At the kitchen door, she looked back. Some of the addicts were stoned and out of it, other were restless, waiting or hoping for a fix.

Blondie squirmed, "Hah! Must be dreaming about something." The Army woman went into the kitchen, still shaking her head.

In Blondie's dream she saw and heard his voice, plain as day. He walked in long strides down the center aisle. He called out something to the woman going through the kitchen doors. She looked him up and down, as she pushed the doors away and said, "Can I help you?"

"I'm looking for somebody, thought she might come here." He stopped but looked around, turning back to the cots filled with people.

"What's your name? Who is it you're looking for?"

He kept turning, and put his hands up in frustration. "I don't know her real name. I... I guess it's Amy, or something like that. I really don't know. I just know that I worry about her. Can't stop worrying. Got to find...don't know where to... Do you have someone here who... who can read? Maybe she isn't...don't know, but I thought..."

"Calm down! If you'll calm down, I'll try to... Wait, you said she can read, didn't you? Maybe it's... wait here." She hurried to Blondie's half-asleep form. He followed her halfway then stopped. He mussed up his hair some more, frantic and uncertain. The Army woman reached down to touch Blondie's shoulder.

Blondie sat up, screaming, "Don't hurt me! Go away! Leave me alone! No, NO! Don't do that! Leave me---" She fell back and turned away, still asleep.

"You can look if you want to, but she's asleep. Don't know who you're looking for, anyway, but you can look, if you think..."

"Can you turn her face this way?"

"Don't know. She was dreaming I guess."

Blondie sat up suddenly. She scratched her tangled hair, "I dreamt it was Mr... don't know..." rubbed her eyes, "Must still be dreaming... can't be."

Meanwhile Ellen, the mother who volunteered, filled her big bathtub with warm water, added bubble bath mix, and gently lowered dirty little Brenda into the bath. Brenda shivered then sat down in the warmth. There were no smiles, the mother noticed. She used to laugh and splash everywhere. "I'd have to hold her to keep her from sliding under the water," Ellen said to herself. Tears fell from her cheeks.

She held one of Brenda's arms to put a warm wet cloth on a knee that needed a good scrub.

Brenda slowly looked at her, then at the washcloth. Looked at the bubbles. Slowly, she smashed an occasional bubble that dared venture too close.

When Ellen washed her hair with baby shampoo, Brenda shook her head, then sat quietly.

Ellen checked the water temperature. It streamed and washed away all the soap. While she was rinsed, Brenda closed her eyes but stayed still. Finally, they were done.

"What have you gone through?" Ellen whispered to herself. Bruised everywhere. One on the side of her face, two more on her back. "What am I to do? Can't even wash her without hurting her."

She gathered Brenda into an over-sized bath towel and went into a room that had stayed the same for over a year. She picked out the largest outfit she could find, still holding her lost and found treasure, still tearing up.

She looked for shoes. All were too small, but socks on clean feet were just fine. Brenda watched.

"The doctor," she said, more to herself than out loud.

"We can go see Dr. Hamilton. He will know what..." she picked up Brenda and went to the hall phone. Sat Brenda beside her to call. Watched Brenda sit without trying to scoot, or walk, away. Brenda looked around but sat where she was put.

Dr. Hamilton could see them later today.

"Does around four-thirty work?"

"Sure" the receptionist answered, "That will be fine."

Her husband will be home by the time we get back. She had called and called. He was still out. She finally left a message that she had a surprise for him.

"I'll leave him a note." She struggled—what could—or what would she tell—she didn't know.

"We will go to Dr. Hamilton's office by four o'clock to be there early". She held Brenda as closely as she dared without making any of the bruises worse.

"Let's have lunch now. Then we'll take a nap."

Brenda said, "Eat."

"Okay. Let's eat." Finally, she laughed. A plan was good. She had a plan.

Ellen started to put Brenda in her crib.

"No, that's for a baby. We need a bigger bed. You are not a baby anymore. We'll get shoes later too. It's naptime now. Let's go to momma's room. This room—is a baby room." Ellen still held her tightly.

Brenda squirmed.

"Oh, am I squeezing you? Sorry I didn't mean to squeeze too much." Ellen laid her down on the big bed and crawled in beside her. She tossed a throw over them both. She couldn't believe that Brenda was beside her. They both slept.

Suddenly, Ellen was awake. What was that noise, she wondered?

"I must have dozed off. I haven't had any sleep for weeks," she mumbled.

Brenda's eyes few open wide. She lay still but turned her head towards Ellen.

"Let's go see," Ellen said. "I thought I heard somebody." She turned to pick up Brenda.

Her husband walked in. "What's this I heard about a surprise?" he said, shedding his coat.

"Oh, Brad. Look!" They found her. They let me—us—keep her," She was rambling. He was stunned.

"Is it really her—I don't know—she's so thin—what are those bruises on her? Come here, little one." He held out his hands to her.

She held tight to Ellen and would not let him touch her. Her face buried inside Ellen's neck, she turned away and trembled, shaking her head as best she could. Clinging.

Ellen tried. She said, "It's Daddy. See, he's glad—surprised—to see you. Can you tell him—maybe she—I'm glad you're home—" tears started again.

Brad hugged her from the back. Brenda clung. She would not look at him.

Sobbing, Ellen said, "I called Dr. Hamilton's office. He can see us after hours. Can you go with us? We need to know—we need to know if she—if she's been—if she is—can you go, too? It's been—"

"Yes, yes, and yes." He said, patting his wife. Can we go now? Do we need to change her?" He sat on the bed, put his hands between his knees and shook his head, bewildered that Brenda was afraid of him.

Ellen and Brenda went into the bathroom. He got up and paced, still confused.

Outside, Ellen tried to put her in the car seat. She wouldn't turn loose. They finally sat together in the back seat. The ride was relatively short but seemed to take hours.

All the patients had gone, The waiting room was empty except for the beaming nurse who came from a hallway with a clipboard in her hands and a smile on her face.

"Come this way, please. Dr. Hamilton is in his office. You can go into his office if you'd like." She held the door to the hallway for them, and said, "Just follow me."

She tried to touch Brenda's hand. The child snatched it away. She hid her hand and turned away obviously afraid.

Dr. Hamilton stood in the doorway to his office, smiling, "Well, well, well. So you're all together again, good to have you here," he said as he looked closely at the clinging child.

"Let's go into an exam room, okay?"

They followed the tall man with only a sprinkle of grey at his temples into a room with only two chairs and a high table that functioned as an exam table.

"Can you put her here?" he said.

Brenda sat on the high table and passively let him listen to her heart. As he shined the light in her eyes, she grabbed the earpieces of his stethoscope and solemnly looked at him. He smiled at her and put the head of the stethoscope on her stomach, guiding the earpieces to her ears.

Her eyes blinked and got rounder, he laughed. "Oh, yes, you have noises inside. Want to hear more? Well, we can move this some and listen to your brave heart. It sounds like rumpty-thump, rump-ty-thump, rumpty-thump." He laughed, she didn't.

"Can you turn her over? On her stomach?"

"I'll try." Ellen whispered, "Maybe."

"Will she let you take off her panties?" He watched the child closely as he showed his stethoscope to Brenda.

Turn her over on her stomach, if you can, and I'll take a look at the bruises on her back.

"It's okay, that's good. Just pull them down, you don't need to take them off. No sign of—." He motioned that the child could sit up if she wanted to.

"Both now or later, you can give her whatever she wants, what-ever she's comfortable with. She is a very good patient."

He stepped away. She lay on her back comfortably.

"Alright, we're all done! Let's head back to my office." Brenda had his stethoscope gripped in her hand with an ear piece dangling in one ear.

After Dr. Hamilton threw away his gloves and washed his hands, he looked at her and laughed, "I'll take those now, thank you." He said, smiling. He sat her up and motioned to Ellen to gather her things. As they walked to his office, he whispered, "There doesn't seem to be any physical evidence of sexual assault, however she has clearly experienced physical and mental trauma. I'll tall you more in my office."

They let the doctor give Brenda a small soft toy to keep her occupied as they settled themselves in the chairs across from the doctor's desk. Once the child seemed to pay them no more attention, he continued.

"Her disposition tells me it's possible she was hit if she cried, so she learned not to cry. As for the bruises, it looks as if she was swung around, more like a rag doll than a real child. Some are deeper than others so you'll want to take care. Keep her diet very balanced and they should heal properly."

They wanted to know if he had any suggestions as to what they could do if they found out who took her.

Carefully shaking his head, he mentioned that such activity was outside his field. He, nonetheless, had one thought.

"If you look for the person or persons who took her, I'd say look for someone who is severely mentally deficient, or—I'm guessing now. Maybe someone who liked to play with dolls but never had one."

He laughed. "That's a real stretch on my part."

He rose and shook hands with the father.

"She is physically sound. With time, she may be okay." He stood and began to walk them toward the door.

"Call me if you need me, but she'll be fine in time. Be patient—as best as you can. Bye Brenda." He waved, she stared but then...her hand outstretched and her fingers opened and closed before she hid against the mother's neck and had both hands hidden.

Brad wrapped his arm around them both as they left.

CHAPTER 8

MR. FIELDS

At the Rec Center, Blondie was still confused. She wiped her eyes, then moved both hands away. She looked back and forth from the familiar woman in the navy-blue long sleeves and a Salvation Army patch where a pocket usually goes, to the strange man.

"Is he with the cops or something? Have I stayed too long and you need the bed for somebody else? Where's the little girl? Did the cops take her? Oh, my head hurts, let me put my shoe on. It's got a hole in it, you know. Oh, my head hurts."

"Shh, shush now. The little girl went with her mother, shh. No, he's not with the cops. He's looking for somebody, shh. Be still now. Just sit still for a minute."

Blondie sat with her knees up. Her elbows on her knees, head in both hands. Her hair was tussled. The blanket fell from her shoulder when she sat up.

With both hands over his mouth, the man gasped.

"It's her," he said behind his hands," I recognize the shirt she wore. Oh, thank goodness, it's her."

She plucked at one sleeve. Looked up at the man, then looked down. Held both hands on her head.

"I thought you were... It's all a dream, I must still be dreaming." She muttered, "Are you here? Can I be awake? No, it's all a... Who are you, anyway. You can't be here, I... was having a ..."

"Shh, shush, shush." The woman kept saying. She looked over at the man.

"Are you sure she's who you're looking for? Oh, mercy. I don't know what to do. Have to ask my super. Gotta be sure. Two in one day. Oh, mercy. I'll be back," She went away to call.

The man watched her go into the kitchen. He watched Blondie pat her forehead with her palm, that did it. He was convinced. Nobody else did that.

Cautiously, he reached down. Said, "Wh..."

"Do you still have magic in your pockets?"

He raised his head. Patted his pocket, and said, "Magic?" Not knowing what she meant. "Oh... yes. Magic," pulled out his phone just as it rang. "Yeah, Eddie here. No, I'm... busy right now. No. I'll talk to you later."

She giggled. Clapped her hands, "I'm not dreaming! You are here!"

She scooted around to stand up, "You sure are tall. Just like before—where is... oh, there she comes. "Yea! Look. He's real."

Confusion came back to her face. "You don't belong here, why are you here?"

He turned away, backed into the wall.

"Guess I was looking for you. Don't ask me why. I... I don't know, but I was."

The Army person came closer, she was slowly and solemnly walking towards them. They looked toward her but didn't say anything.

"My super was out." She said, "I didn't leave a message. Called back three times. Guess I'm on my own. Will—what's to do, I need the cot. Guess you can go, if'n you wanta. Don't know."

"Go—where to?" Blondie muttered, confused, she brightened, "Yes, go to the bathroom. I'll go now." She walked, unsteadily past and headed toward the back, head held high, thumping her palm against her forehead.

"Go after her, please." The man said, frantic.

The Army woman took after Blondie, "Oh no, she'll be all wet again. Oh, no!" She turned back to the man as she hurried, "See what you've done!" She said over her shoulder as she opened the door with the skirted woman on it.

Blondie was not in the shower. A pair of feet and ragged jeans was in one of the stalls.

"I've got more to do than chase after you." The woman yelled and leaned against a sink. She crossed her arms.

"Are you mad at me?" Blondie smiled as she closed the door to the stall. The woman moved so Blondie could wash her hands and face. The long braid was pulled and the torn piece was tightened.

The woman said, "Come on!" She left, Blondie followed. She stuck out her tongue at someone they passed who had sat up to watch what was going on.

"What's his name—I forgot. Can't remember—"

"You must know his name! He's looking for you!" The woman said, impatient. "Guess I'll just decide on my own. Here, take her. Nobody else cares, I guess." She looked at Blondie, sighed and walked away, shaking her head.

At the kitchen door, she paused. Wiped her eyes with the corner of her shirt and went inside.

The man didn't know what to do. He started to say something when the phone in his pocket rang. Blondie laughed. She hung her head. Put one hand against her mouth. Kept giggling.

"What is it?" he angrily said into the phone. "No, I said I was busy. No!" he hung up and jammed the phone back into his pocket. "Come on," he said to Blondie. She giggled and followed him.

At the front, he stopped, looked at her and then shook his head. "Stay here, I'll find the car." She stayed, uncertain. She shifted from one foot then the other. Slapped her forehead over and over with her fingers splayed.

A car screeched at the curb. He jumped out, leaving his door open. Ran to open the passenger door and went to get Blondie.

"Come, on" he said. She hesitated, "Come on," he said again. Ran to open the Rec Center's door for her. "Let's go."

She shook her head, "Don't know where."

"Doesn't matter. You will be..." He didn't know either, he realized. Paused, then said, "We'll go to Bella. Yes, that's it. We'll go to Bella."

"Bella... don't know Bella." She got in the car. Looked around as he closed the passenger door and ran around to get inside.

She wasn't afraid. She looked and looked. Smiled. Pointed. Looked and looked.

"I can read, you know." Finally, she settled in for a quiet ride, she smiled and said, "Yessiree. I can read." He drove.

CHAPTER 9

BELLA

He pulled the car into a driveway, next to a bungalow style house, with a wide front porch that had three steps leading up to it.

Pink and red roses bloomed against the porch.

"Rose... a rose by any name. Can it smell so sweet—that's not right." She stopped. "I can't get it right..."

He went up the steps, disheveled. "Did you say something?"

He didn't wait for an answer. He opened the big wooden door instead, then turned around.

Blondie was still standing on the sidewalk gazing at the rose hedge, scratching her head. She sang, "Ring around the rosie..."

"Come on." He said.

She slowly walked up the steps. Saw the green double swing on one side of the porch. She ran to it. Sat down, patted it then pushed it a bit. Said, "Wheeee!..." She rocked back and forth, smiling.

Standing in the open door, he called, "Bella, it's me."

Bella, a middle aged stocky woman with curly grey hair came from the back of the house drying her hands on a cloth.

"Oh, Mr. Fields. You're home early. I was just fixing... what is it? You're... your hair is all... here, sit down before you... what is the matter?"

He went back to the porch, holding the door. Looked at Blondie. She was happily pushing herself in the swing, singing to herself.

He turned back to Bella, "I brought somebody," he said. "She's on the porch." He rubbed his tousled hair, and kept looking back through the door.

"Somebody?" Asked Bella.

"I don't know what to do." He was pacing, filled with uncertainty.

Bella looked out the door. She saw a pretty girl with a rag that tied back long blonde hair. She wore torn jeans and a too-big shirt. For some reason, the girl was humming to herself and gently pushing the swing back and forth while she was grinning. Her shoes had no laces in them and were too dirty for humans to wear. So were her arms. Dirty was hardly the description for such a pretty young girl.

"One of the homeless? You brought one of the homeless?" she asked as she confronted him.

He sat down. Held his head. Nodded, then looked up at Bella.

"Is she destructive?" asked Bella as she twisted the cloth in her hands, "Or maybe an addict? She's a mess."

He jumped up, "No, no. She's never destructive—at least s far as I know." He hesitated. Looked outside briefly.

Turned back, looked at Bella, and said smiling, "She's more like a puppy. She dances around, giggles and forgets where she is." He paused then looked at Bella.

"No. She's not destructive at all, not that I've ever seen at least." He peeked out the door again.

"I just don't know what's to become of her... she can't live on the streets! It's too dangerous!"

Bella had gone into the dining room, off the front room, pulled out one of the heavy chairs and sat down. She held the cloth against her face—thinking.

He repeated, "She can't live on the streets! She's too pretty!"

Bella turned, "But she can't stay here, either. You have to work. Besides, a grown man and a street urchin. It won't... it won't be... seemly."

"But she's a child trapped in a woman's body!" he slumped. "What's to become of..."

Blondie came in though the open door.

"What's to become of who?" she asked. "You're Mr. Fields, I remember now." She clapped her hands, held them together like a prayer.

She turned to Bella, "Oh, hello. Who are you? Do you live here? I like your roses. I have a hole in my shoe, do you want to see?" She sat on the floor. Took off her shoe and held it up with her fingers poked through.

Bella put both hands over her mouth, then laughed. "Here child. You can sit in a chair." She held out one hand. She turned his way and quietly said, "I see what you mean."

Blondie got up and hopped to an overstuffed chair. She patted the big arms, looked at them each with a turn of her head and grinned.

"Is this your chair? It has flowers on it. I don't much like to sit on flowers. They mostly go outside." She got up. Brushed off the seat of the chair. Stood with her hands behind her back, grinning.

"Well, it has been a nice visit. Sorry, I have to go. Thank you... Sorry, I didn't... What did you say your name was... I'll go now. " She started to leave almost in tears. She began holding her head high as she reached the door.

Mr. Fields jumped up, "Wait. You don't have to leave. We'll—" he looked at Bella.

Bella got up and walked toward her, "Do you want to sit on the swing some more? It's a good strong swing. We will go into the other room for just a minute. You will wait for us, yes? That's a good girl. Wait in the swing. We will be right back, okay?"

Bella nodded to her employer to go to the dining room. "Wait now," she said to Blondie. "Mr. Fields will be right here. You will sit in the swing now, yes? Good, good, good! Yes, sit in the swing."

Back in the house, she led with a shake of her head to Fields, "Come to the dining room. She can't hear us in there," she said and sat down in the same straight chair she had been in before.

He followed. Still rumpled and confused. After he sat a while, he raised his head, "You have an idea?"

"Sort of an idea. It may not work. We'll see."

"Oh, Bella, it has to be better than any I have thought of. Come on, out with it. You already said that she can't live on the street with the viruses, addicts, sex mongers and all. What can I do?"

"Well—I have a sister. She is by herself now. She had a bad fall last summer and walks with a cane, I worry about her."

"Yes? Yes, go on."

"Well—she may—she may not—like the notion that she needs help. All that big farm she tries to tend. All by herself in the country. What do you think—do you think the girl will go and, will she be suitable, and will my sister go along with—"

"We'll call her." He perked up, then stood up, "We'll ask. It won't hurt!" He ran out to the front porch.

Blondie was nowhere near the swing that still swayed. Frantic, he walked back and forth with one hand on his mouth. He leaned against a post, then sat on a porch rail looking up and down the street. He heard humming below him.

She was patting each rose below him. He crumpled with relief. After catching himself, he ran down the steps to the side yard and came to a halt in front of her. She smiled, "Ring around the Rosie... don't know the rest!" she stopped.

"Uh... Want to take a ride now?" he asked. He tried to act composed. "First, we have to see Bella. If it's okay with her, then we'll go for a ride. If you want to," he added

"Bella," she nodded. "Goodbye, pretty roses." She waved with her fingers opening and closing, then followed him up the steps.

Bella stood near the open door, nodding.

"I talked with Amelia Margot. She said to come on. Here are directions, I'll finish up here. Now go. Goodbye little one."

"You are his mother," Blondie said.

Bella laughed, "No, child. I'm his housekeeper. You go now and see Amelia Margot. You will like her." Her fingers were crossed behind her.

During the car ride, Blondie stared out the window. She was scrunched up against the door, taking in the building that went past.

"I usta have a car, you know," She finally said.

He almost ran a red light he was so surprised. He looked toward her as his brakes squealed. "Boy am I glad the car behind us stopped in time, that's a relief."

"Relief? Are you shocked I had a car? Don't know what happened to it... don't know..." After struggling with her seatbelt that got too tight with the sudden stop, she went back to the door and stared at the outside some more.

"Do you want to know where we are going?" he finally asked as he slowed down a bit.

"For a ride, you said." She finally answered, "We're going for a ride. In a car."

After a while, the buildings got farther and farther apart. More hills. More trees. More silence between the two passengers.

Blondie began to wriggle.

"Do you want to stop someplace?" he asked.

"Stop, yes. Can we stop now?"

He laughed, "We can stop when we get to a gas station. You can look for one, then we'll stop."

"A gas station? You mean one of those places that have flying horses on top?"

"One of those will be fine. Yes, one of those." He smiled, "You can use the bathroom there."

"Do I have to take a bath, too?"

"No, no." he answered and smiled again, "Just be on the look-out, okay?"

"Your car smells good. It smells like you, you know."

He shook his head, the change of subject didn't surprise him after he'd had the experience with the burgers, but it still threw him a bit.

"I'll go inside and get us a few things to nibble on while I pay for the gas. Do you want anything, like candy or chips? Anything else?"

She shook her head slowly.

"Look! Behind the trees! There! I see a red horse, behind the trees! Up in the air! Look!"

"Yes, I see it. We'll leave the highway, turn left and find Pegasus, the flying horse."

Blondie clapped her hands and sat straighter. She was excited to have been helpful.

"Pegasus, usta read about Pegasus... I can read, you know."

They stopped. She flew out of the car as he pulled up to a pump.

"Woah. You may have to go inside and ask for a key." She was running, the long, ragged shirt-tail flying behind, but she heard him and stopped. She shifted from one foot then the next. Finally, she said, "Okay." And took off running again.

The place was busy. The man behind the counter saw her and pointed to the back. She kept going until she saw the lady's skirt cut-out on the door.

When she came out, she saw him putting the gasoline hose back into the pump. "They have a hot air machine in there." She said. "I washed my hands and face. Pushed the big button! Hot air felt good. Almost dried my hands and arms. See?" She held up her hands and turned them in every direction, "Redid my plait... or braid... or whatever it's called." She turned all around for him to see.

He laughed, "I'll be right back. Go sit in the car and wait, okay?"

"Okay," She pranced to the car, still proud of herself. Most of the bruises gone. She touched her bottom lip. Still only a little bit swollen, "Be gone soon," she muttered to herself.

A bag almost hid his face when he came to the car. She was sitting there, no longer scrunched against the door.

"I didn't do the thing around me." She said. "Don't know how it works." She held up the seat belt.

"Here. Take this. I'll fix it," he said as he handed over the bag and reached for the black straps.

As he slid behind the wheel, he punched in the seatbelt as she explored the bag.

"Oh, goodie! There's all sorts of stuff in here," she exclaimed as she held up a small bag of chips.

Several smaller bags and bars spilled across her lap and legs as she giggled. "Where are we going now? Can I eat some of this? Why is there so much? Did you leave anything out? Did you? Do you want some?" She kept a monolog going.

He sat and laughed, glad she was okay with his purchases.

"Yes," he said. He tightened the seatbelt but was glad she was not against the door. "You can eat anything or everything you want," he said as he cautiously turned the car around and went back to the highway.

She ripped open a small package of chips, stuffed her mouth after gingerly sampling one.

"Where to now?" she asked with cheeks puffed out like a squirrel and both hands picking up the remnants of what she had dropped on her side of the car.

"Oh. This is tight!" The seatbelt pulled her back, keeping her from reaching what she'd dropped on the floor. "Guess it wants to stay down there. Oh, well." She sat back upright.

He hesitated, then said, "We're going to the country. We'll meet Bella's sister. You remember Bella?"

"Oh, yes, Bella. She had roses. A swing on a porch. She's your..." patted her forehead, then said, "Don't know..."

"Bella is my housekeeper. She has a sister, Amelia Margot, who lives outside of town. In the country. You'll like her."

Puzzled, Blondie talked to herself, repeating what he'd said, but no words came out of her mouth. She stopped eating.

Finally, she said, "Why?"

CHAPTER 10

AMELIA MARGOT

After a few more miles, Mr. Fields turned onto a small dirt road. At the end of the road, Blondie saw a rambling white house with a screened porch on one side. He parked near the porch.

Slowly, he turned toward Blondie and said, "We're here."

She surprised him when she said, "Look! There are lots of roses in the front. It's like Bella's."

Relieved, he laughed. "Yes. Like Bella's"

A tall, slim brunette with salt and pepper hair pulled back, came down the two steps from the screened porch. Walking slowly with the help of a cane, she went to the car as Mr. Fields got out.

"Welcome. Bella called. She said you were coming." A smile lighted her face.

Blondie got out of the car. As she noticed the cane, she asked, "Are you crippled?

The tall lady laughed. "No. I'm just a little unsteady. Come on in, I'm..."

"If you aren't crippled, do you always need a cane? What does 'unsteady" mean? Do you... Are you... " Blondie shook her head and followed them, frowning.

They chatted, careful to keep their voices low. Occasionally they both looked at Blondie.

Mr. Fields held the screened door open for all of them to enter the porch.

Blondie stood still near the door. They waited for her to speak. She finally broke her silence. "Oh, look! She has benches on both sides of that long table! It's just like Mama's." Her hand flew to her mouth as she realized she'd said something out loud. Looking back and forth to the two adults, she wanted to disappear.

They tried not to laugh as they both smiled. They didn't want her to think they were making fun of her.

"You have both been in the car so long, I'd ask you to come on in and take a chair, but maybe you'd rather see the outside of the place."

"Anything you suggest, "Mr. Fields answered. "Is that okay with you, Blondie?"

Suddenly shy, she just nodded and played with her long braid. She pulled it over one shoulder and tried to fix the tie-back on it.

The opposite side of the porch had a second door. While Blondie fiddled with her hair, they left and walked toward a large barn out back. When they realized Blondie was not with them, they stopped and turned. Mr. Fields called her.

"Are you coming?"

While they waited, they talked softly like old friends, still smiling.

Blondie shook herself out of her funk and ran down the two steps at the back of the porch and came to a halt at the two of them. She looked first at one, then at the other. She stopped at Amelia Margot.

Blurting out, she asked, "Do you have a name? I don't always want to call you Bella's sister, do I? What's your ordinary name? I can read, you know."

They got quiet at her outburst. First, they looked at her then at each other. Neither knew what to say or to do.

Amelia Margot saved the moment. Patiently, she said, "Amelia Margot is what almost everyone calls me. You can. . .Wait. What is your name? I don't know that either."

Blondie ignored the question of her own name and instead said over and over, "Amelia Mar. . .Amelia Mar. . Can I just call you Amee? That's almost like my own real name." Shy again, Blondie turned around and around slowly. She kept repeating "Amee, Amee, Amee."

As quickly as she started, she stopped. "That's almost like my own name. Maybe my real name is Amy, don't know. Sounds right, so that must be it. Amy, Amy, Amy.

Two sounds. Both alike." She clapped her hands.

"Two Amys. That's pretty good. You are real pretty and Mr. Fields is real good. He bought a really big sack of good stuff for us to eat on the way here!"

"We can go inside now, if that's okay. I need to make a few calls. Then I'll have a drink if that suits everyone, I mean."

The two Amys followed Mr. Fields as they started toward the house. Blondie turned round and round as she walked. She kept saying Amee, Amee, Amee. On one of the walk arounds, she spotted the tree.

"Oh, my! That's the biggest tree I ever saw!" She ran toward the tree, yelling. "Look! Look! There's a swing on that lowest limb. It's made to fit two people. I never saw a swing on a tree before. Look!" She ran to the swing.

In front of a huge barn, she finally reached the tree. She pushed the green swing a bit then caught it and sat, holding the chains to go back and forth.

She called to the two people who stopped to watch and smile at her. "Like Bella's porch swing!" she yelled. "Whee. This is good." She turned loose of both chains to pat herself on the forehead as the swing went higher.

She fell out.

Mr. Fields started to run toward her to pick her up. Amelia Margot put a hand on this arm to hold him back. She shook her head. With his mouth open and beginning to say something, he stayed where he was. They waited but were restless.

The gently moving swing bumped Blondie's head. She twisted around and caught the swing. As she climbed up to sit down, she patted the seat beside her. She held one hand on her head and said. "I'm not made at you, nice

Swing. It's my own fault. I turned loose."

She sat silently a few minutes, holding her head with one hand. Finally, set her feet on the bare spot on the ground. After getting her balance, she looked at the two who were waiting for her and laughed.

She clapped her hands and went toward them still smiling. "I took a flip," she said.

"You sure did," said Mr. Fields. "Are you all set for another performance, or will you come to the house with us?"

She stopped. "Performance? I used to perform. . .somewhere. . .it was dark. . .She stomped her foot. Oh, pooh! She tossed her head, went up the two steps to open the screened door by herself and led the others inside. They smiled as they followed her.

Inside the kitchen, Amelia Margot fixed sweetened tea for herself and Amy. She mixed a drink for Mr. Fields from her late husband's hidden stash. She pointed to the ladder-back kitchen chairs around the large wooden table and told Amy, "Choose any chair you want. Have a seat."

Blondie stood still to look around. "Do you cook?"

"Sometimes."

"How come there are square things on the table if you don't cook?"

Those are cheese cakes. I baked them in the oven early this morning. Do you want one? Help yourself."

Blondie shook her tousled head. Wandered around. Touched the enamel counter on the tall cabinet near a window. There were doors on the top and bottom of the cabinet with a drop-in strainer behind the biggest drawer.

"Mama had something like this. Her's hada bin for flour be-hind...or in...one of the bottom doors. It was yellow, not green... don't 'member.

Mr. Fields stood away from the place where he was leaning. "Best be going." He walked the few steps toward Blondie. "Do you want to stay here? Would you be happy to stay with Amelia Margot?"

"Her? Her name is Amee. How long? When will you be back? You will come back? How long? Mama said it was something like a Hoosier...don't 'member. She bit her nail across from the bruised side of her mouth. "You will..." she was still looking at the cabinet.

She could see them talking out the window. He held her hand, kissed her cheek, then got in the car and started it. He turned the car around on the wide path, and was gone.

"Guess I'll stay," she said out loud. Oh, well. Everybody goes. Guess he wouldn't stay either. At least it'd not raining." She went to the table and sat in one of the tall straight chairs.

"Humph! Two names. Almost the same. Wonder what's in that shed next to the big tree?" She mumbled as she looked at the cheese cakes. "Bet she cooks. We'll see."

"Well!" Amelia Magot said on her return. She propped her cane on the back of the chair across from Blondie and sat down. "Guess you and I will be room-mates. Whatever Bella wants, Bella gets." She laughed.

Blondie tucked her head down. "Bella wanted me to come see you. Bella has roses. Bella has a swing on her front porch. Bella has... "

"Yes, yes, yes. Do you want to change clothes now? Do you... Guess you don't have other clothes, do you?"

"No clothes. Blondie sat straighter. "Sam. . . don't know where Sam went. Sam gave me his shirt." She giggled. "It's kinda big. So is...was...Sam. I don't know."

"Well. We will see. Except for my being taller, you and I are about the same size. Let's go look." Amelia Margot got up. "Come on. Let's go look. We'll see."

Blondie's eyes got wider and wider as they went through the house to a back bedroom. She had never seen so many rooms or so many doors. There were doors to bathrooms, closets, bedrooms, and even to a small office. She lost count even though she had to open and to gaze inside most of them. Soft laughs came from Amelia Margot as she walked slowly or waited for Amy. She stood beside one door and ushered Amy inside. "What size do you wear? Do you know?"

A shoulder shrug was all Blondie managed as an answer. "I have new sox," she said. "The Army lady at the center gave me new sox." She hopped off one of her shoes. "Oh, my. Seems to be dirty now," she said and held up one sneaker. "Has a hole in it," she said as she poked a finger through the hole. She wiggled her finger and giggled.

Lifting clothes on hangers from the large double closet, Amelia Margot turned to see Blondie's finger stuck through the bottom of her shoe. They both laughed. She flung the clothes on the bed.

Amelia Margot said, "See if any of these suit you. Or, if any of them fit. Take your pick." She smiled.

"I've never seen so many clothes except maybe in a store. Didn't know anybody to have so many. Can't wear them all at once, unless it gets real cold. Maybe not even then. How can. . . Are you sure about this?"

"You try them on, one at a time, then choose what you like. Just pitch what you have on now out the door and I'll wash them for you. Okay?" She started toward the door. "Oh, wait. I almost forgot." She went to the tall chest in a corner, opened two different drawers and grabbed some filmy things.

"Here are some underwear. Choose what you want. I'll be back." The door closed behind her.

"I'm dirty. How can anybody put on these fine clothes when they are dirty?" Dirty or not, she managed to shed the over-sized shirt and the ragged jeans. Then came off one shoe and two socks. Her knees were scabbed from being scooted against rocks and rough concrete. She rubbed them.

Clad in only her stained tee and an old pair of panties, the looked around. She went to a mirror a frosted glass rim around it and found a door beside it. She opened it.

"Oh goodie. A bathroom!" Inside, she found a jar of bubble bath, a fluffy towel, and a soft white robe that was hanging on the back of the door. "Oh my! It's a palace! Well, I'll be swarmy! There's a big tub plus a fancy-dan shower. Humph! Can't have a scruffy, tattered and torn thing in this fine place. Guess it's calling me!"

She turned the two fancy knobs on the bathtub. Soon the water was warm enough for her to use half of the bottle of bubble bath. It made lots of bubbles.

In she slid, half-dressed with her tee-shirt still on. The ragged ribbon, torn from the long shirt was still on her pig-tail braid. A sigh escaped as she lay back.

With quiet steps, Amelia Margot opened the bathroom door and stood over the child/woman.

"Guess I'll have to help," she said, shaking her head. She took the soft robe off the back of the door and spread it like a curtain. In a sweet voice, she shouted to the one sleeping. "It's time to get out of the water. It's cold now."

Blondie's eyes flew open. It took her a white to realize where she was. After wiping her eyes, she muttered, "Sorry."

"Shed all your clothes and leave them in the tub. I'll get them after the water drains out. You can put of this robe that I'm holding then you can see if any of the clothes I got out fit you.

As soon as Blondie put one arm in and held onto the rest of the robe, Amelia Margot left, saying "I'll be back."

In the bedroom, Amelia Margot sorted underwear into one pile. In another, she put jeans. The last stack was various shirts, both short and long sleeved.

Out came Blondie. Wet hair was splayed across her shoulders, dripping over the terry cloth robe that swallowed her but was tied tight around her middle.

Smiling, Amelia Margot pointed toward the bathroom. "There's a towel in there if you want to wrap it around your head," she said.

A blank stare greeted her, but Blondie went back to fetch a towel. She came out trying to pack her wet hair into it.

"Here. Let me help you. First, try out the underwear. Second, if the jeans are too long, we will fix that. Then, help yourself to which ever shirt suits your taste. Now, I'll fix you up with a turban for your hair." She tied the towel around Blondie's hair, patted it, took her cane and left.

"She sure is happy. Whatever that means. Guess not being without anything to eat does that to a soul. Oh, well. Never had a turban before. It sure is something'. Keeps things in place I guess. Oh, well. Here goes. Gotta pick out sumpthin I guess. Brrr. Sure is cold without any clothes."

When Amelia Margot returned, she was greeted by a silent gut fully dressed young woman. Jeans covered two bare feet that hung off the bed. The wet towel no longer covered half-dried hair that fell loose. The towel was slung over a bed post.

"Well now. Let's turn up the cuffs. Do you like short cuffs or tall cuffs?"

Shoulders went up as hands went out.

"Okay. Let's try tall ones," Amelia Margot offered.

As she tucked the long jean bottoms into tall cuffs, Blondie stared but stayed silent.

"Next, the sleeves need to be rolled up so they won't look too long. You can do that. Then we can have lunch.

Come this way. We'll find sox and shoes later. What size shoes do you wear? Don't know? No problem. We'll see about that later. Anyway, I'll get the laundry and take it to the washing machine on our way. Right now, let's go get lunch!"

Blondie wiggled her freed toes, jumped off the bed, and followed her new room-mate down the hall while she rubbed down her front and patted her new sleeves.

The door slammed shut just as blondie went inside. Pitch black darkness greeted them. Amee found the two lanterns by feel. She handed one to Blondie, "Don't know how these work. Maybe you can figure it out. Never had to use them. Maybe they will light. Don't know."

"You sound like me." Blondie laughed. "I don't know too." She said and fiddled with the lantern in the dark.

Along with howling wind and a slamming porch doors they though a voice called. "let me in!" More pounding the voice sounded closes. "Open the door! Let me in."

"Here, Amee. Take the lantern. I'll try to push open that heavy door. Somebody's out there."

Using muscles she didn't know she had Blondie pushed and grunted. Nothing badged. She turned around on the same platform inside and used her legs to push. The door gave a crack. Fingers gripped edges and pulled it widely. From outside, a small body dripping with rain dived inside. It feel on top of Blondie.

Untangling arms and legs, she said "Tommy! What are you doing? Why are you outside in a storm? Get off me!" He rolled down the steps. Bumped into Amelia Margot holding two lanterns. "'Scuse me, Ma'am. Sure is dark in here." "You wanted to know how come I'm here. Well, I was up at the next farm helping get their tractor started. Didn't do no good. The motor's froze. When the big blow started, they sent me on home. Didn't make it; 'Membered helpin' your husband dig this here shelder. I was a little kid then. "He took a breath, then continued. "Well, so, here I am. Sure is dark in here. Don't you have no light, Ms. Amelia Margot?"

Amee showed the two lights at him, then, Blondie added; "Since you are so good at fixin's things, see if you can make those lanterns work! She thought he bragged too much.

"Huma. Well, they are kinda rusty on their handles. Must be battery run. How long they been in here?

Amee said, "I brought them in last week when I put watermelon pickles on the shelves, the battery should still be good but since I left the doors open then I don't know how to turn them on or where the switches are."

He fumbled with both lanterns. One came on, the other glimmered then went out. "One has lost the big button that went to the front. Maybe you can find it later. "He set the lantern down. "Boy, that wind is howling. Momma must be worried about me. Sure hope she and the girls are okay. Sure do."

They lost track of time. It was a long time, but not nearly as long as it seemed. Finally both the wind and the rain let up. The door was opened and three escaped. They were tense, damp and muddy albeit grateful. Blondie still carried the basket of eggs. Tommy half ran behind Blondie saying, "Thanks, thanks for getting' that door open. Gotta go." He took off.

Amee turned off the lantern, picked up here cane, and slowly went up the steps. Sadly she said, "we'll look around later. Frist we need to check on Mr. Gregory."

In the wind-whipped barn, Mr. Gregory stood in his stall, shivering. Amee took him an apple she had found on the ground. Then she covered him with an old blanket that had blown around his feet.

She stroked his nozzle and hugged him while she whispered softly in his mane. Blondie watched. She didn't know what to do.

On the way back to the house, they stopped to stare. Small limbs were everywhere along with leaves and whatever was not tied down. The swing's chains were tangled and wrapped around its solitary limb. There was no sign of the swing.

"We can look for the swing later. First, we need to wash off the mud and change our clothes," Amee said.

Blondie followed her. Still numb. At the porch, they stopped. All the screen-wire was torn away from their uprights which were splintered or missing. The long table was outside. It rested on it's top, upside down. The two long benches were scattered. One was on its side, halfway on the parch and halfway tilted against the outside wall.

What was left of the screen-wire was flapping or else rolled up to the top of the porch. "We can't do anything about anything just yet. "Amee quietly said, "just be grateful it's a strong house."

The basket of eggs were put on the counter the women walked like zombie to their rooms to get rid of mud. After warm baths and dry clothes they were ready to go out again. The phone rang.

Standing on the wind-strewn porch. Blondie heard her say, "He's fine. Has been in the storm shelter with us. He should be there shortly

- are you and the girls safe? - - - good. We'll talk later." Putting the benches against the house, Blondie waited. Amee came to the porch. Shook her head, "Let's go see about the garden."

Blondie tried to straighten the back screened door which barely held on two things. She helped Amee down the two concrete steps and followed her. Only vines remained where once tomatoes grew. Stakes for the running beans were flattened or broken off at the ground. A few stubborn beans clung to the vines, ready to be picked.

Puddles rested where once something had been planted. They were too shaken to do anything except look at the mess. "Let's see about the hen house. There may... Amee both wanted and didn't want to see anything else.

"Oh, look! There's the swing." Blondie ran toward the far wall where the heavy machinery was partially sheltered. She moved the slanted swing that was full of leaves from its resting place. "A car! There's a car here! I didn't know you had a car! Does it still run?

Oh my! It looks pretty good. Can you drive it?" She prattled on. Brushing leaves from it and from the swing as she kept pulling debris. "Let's drive." Blondie patted her head turned toward Amee. "That was then. This is now." She said and lifted one end of the swing. "It's heavy. Can it do it by itself."

Amee smiled, "Yes. But we can do more later. Now it's time to..." "To see what we need to do." Blondie interrupted, "One thing then the other, right?"

"Yes. But I think that saying is, first one thing, then another. Something like that. You are right. What do we do first?"

"Eat leftovers?"

That got the first real laugh she'd had since she fell in the mud puddle and come up with half her face covered with mud. "Okay. Let's go find some left overs."

They walked together hand in hand for the first time.

CHAPTER 11

Mama

"Mama always grew radishes. They grow real fast. First thing, she'd wait 'till the ground was just right. Had to be a little bit damp but not wet. "Blondie turned some over with her triangle hoe. "This soaks dry 'nough, what you think? I'll just sprinkle some of these lil' tiny seed."

"That is fine. That's the longest time you've ever talked about anything." Amee said. Propped on her cane, she watched. "Mama could grow anything. She didn't have a big garden like this here. But she growed cabbages when it was cool. Even had some rows of popcorn. They're not as tall as real corn. She growed them too." Blondie kept strowing the little seed. She wanted a long row to fill in what was left of the garden.

"Glad you kept these pockets of seed." She crumpled the paper pockets and stuffed them into a socket of her jeans. Brushed by hands together. "What do we do now?"

"Don't know. Guess we can try squash. How's about summer squash? I've got some left in the freezer, but fresh would be good later." Amee dug some seed from her apron pocket.

"Then can we go fix the swing?"

"Let's make the hills for the squash. Five flat seed to a hill, then we'll go fix the swing. Looks like I may have enough of their flat seed to do about six hills. That should be enough."

"If there's some egg shells around, we can put some in these hills as you call 'em. Supposed to feed the plants and keep squirrels away. They don't like the sharp edges of the shells. Haven't seen any squirrels, they must like cities. Don't like cities much. Too much concrete. No place to rest."

She looked at Amee. "Let's fix the swing now."

The swing drug away from the shed just fine. Blondie tugged it by one arm rest. Amee used her cane to try to unwind the chains from the limb. "There's a ladder in the barn. If you can get it, the chains may come down. There's some tools you may need also", Amee told her young helper.

"I found it! Got some tools, too." Amee heard. With the barn door open, there was plenty of light.

The horse stood still. He munched at his feed box. "humph! Amee must have come out here real early while I slept." She said softly for her words not to disturb Mr. Gregory.

The ladder rested against the tree. Blondie managed to unwind the twisted chains without any slapping against her as she threaded them down.

"mama fixed everything and anything. Don't know what all she could do when she set her head to it", she told Amee. "that is, when she wasn't painting and drawing pictures. She could sew too. Sewed up a storm. Made me dresses. Oh, mama's gone. They didn't tell me." Growing quite, she stopped fiddling with the chains. Shook her head. Seemed to be listening to some far away voice.

One hand held to her mouth, Amee put her forefinger to signal for more silence. Her ands then here held with palms outward. Head turned for listening both way.

At last she said, "I hear a car."

Slowly the car turned into ruts where once there was gravel.

A door opened before the car stopped at the end of what had been a secure driveway.

Out flew Tommy, running toward the two women. Once the car stopped at the end of what had been a screened porch, Mr. Fields carefully got out. He held onto the open door of the car and took his time follow Tommy.

"whatcha doing? I can fix that! No need to climb a ladder. Come on. I'll always show ya."

With one last loop of chain, Blondie slowly climbed off the ladder.

Well, well, well. If it's not the wonder kid. He can fix anything. See if you can fix this then." She put her hands on her hips, daring him to try.

"Okay, Miss Prissy. You sure are pretty!" he said and picked up a chain to look at it.

She noticed Mr. Fields. Patted her hair down. Straightened and tightened her braid. Waved at him and watched Amee slowly walk toward him for a hug.

"So. Fix it then."

"Get any big eyebolts?"

"What's that?"

"To fix the chains onto the arms, Ninny!"

"Don't know. Look in the tool box in that barn, you're so smart, you'll know what you're looking for if'n you can find 'em."

He walked toward the big sturdy barn.

"this door is whonky too. Won't hang right 'less it's fixed. I'll see to it later."

He had on shoes, too big for him, she noticed. Mama said we were not to wear somebody else's shoes. Might have germs. Mama's gone. She kept her thoughts to herself and waited.

Mr. Fields and Amee, arms intertwined, came toward her.

"And how are you?" he asked.

Suddenly shy, Blondie nodded. "Okay", she whispered.

"You girls surely have a lot of work to do. Amee planted something I see."

Spoken like a trooper, Amee said, "Oh, Amy did all that. She's a good helper like you said, she'd be. She's fine company too."

You talked...

She didn't finish the sentence. Got quiet. With a handful of tools, Tommy joined them and proudly put tools in a row on the swing's seat. He looked at Blondie but didn't say a word. Just started his fixing."

Blurted out, Blondie said, "Mama thought idle hands were the devil's doing."

Twisted toes in a dirt pile, Blondie kept talking. "Mama was sweet. Everybody liked her. Liked her cooking too. The cakes she made were bigger and taller than most." Silence settled over her.

"Mama's gone. Don't know where. Nobody told me." Blondie turned away.

Tommy looked at her. Turned back to his work, but shook his head.

Mr. Fields walked to her. He started to put his arms around her but stopped. His hands went into his pockets instead.

"Uhmm", he cleared his throat. "I looked up your mother. She had a big send off. People came from miles around to the church. The front yard was full. Standing room only inside at her funeral."

Turned around, she looked up. "you found mama? How'd you find mama?"

"Well", he thought a while. "one of my suppliers took pictures. He was there."

"Oh mama." Blondie patted her forehead with the palm of her hand. "Musta slept a longtime", she muttered.

Amee and Mr. Fields looked at each other. Amee shook her head. Signaled to let her go on.

Tommy kept on working. His head down. Straight and determined, Blondie looked at both Mr. Fields and at Amee. She walked around a bit then faced them both. "Well, this is now. That was then. Mama always... will, almost always... said to forget the past if we could. Then... then look at the tomorrows. Oh, mama! I miss her so much!"

She ran to both. Amee and Mr. Fields. Hugged them quickly then ran to the house.

CHAPTER 12

Eddie Fields

Blondie sat on the edge of the bed with her hands dangling between her legs. A vacant stare lent a stoney feature to her pale face.

Footsteps. It sounded like they were coming down the hall. Was it one person or two?

Mr. Fields must be with Amee, Blondie thought. "Oh well. That's the way it is."

Blondie got up. She went to the bathroom and let down her braid on the way. She splashed water on her face and stood looking at herself in the mirror.

"Mama...why does the pain keep coming and going?" she asked to no one. Holding onto the edge of the sink, she picked up the green plastic handle of the brush and started brushing her hair.

"At least I can brush my hair!" she said and laughed. "Now I have clean clothes and sleep in a real bed. Besides, I'm not picked on anymore just because I'm broken. And... there's no more always looking over my shoulder on trying to sleep on hard concrete.

She slammed the brush against the counter.

"but everybody goes away. They leave me!" she sat on the edge of the bed.

"Well, not everybody. Amee's still here but Mr. Fields came to see Amee."

Footsteps sounded in the hallway again. One pair this time. She jumped up, took the brush, and ran into the bedroom. She sat on the edge of the bed again, the brush, the brush still in one hand with her hair spread over her shoulders.

Despondent, she sat and stared at nothing. He was gone.

After a long time, she thought she heard a sound. She stood up to hear better.

"Just the house, squeaking." She said, listening.

"No, that was footsteps". Wondering who might be in the hall, she put an ear to the door. "Glad I've still got this brush in my hand", she held the brush handle harder. Looked around. Saw nothing else that looked like a weapon.

Footsteps came to her door. She stepped back, waited and frightened.

Softly three raps sounded against the door. The bed was in her way. She moved backwards until she fell against the bed and sat down shivering.

The door was unlocked. It opened. In came Mr. Fields who turned and closed the door behind him.

He turned to look at her. Decided to ignore the frightened glance he get and said, "I went out to see how Tommy and the swing were getting along. He's clever that boy."

"He can't read", she blurted.

"Yes, I know. Can happen to anyone whose letters move around or are in switched places from time to time. It's very unsettling. As far as I know, it is very difficult. Doesn't mean he can't do other things though. Shall we go see?"

He held out his hand to her. She looked at his hand and then shook her head.

"No", she said.

"Is that a 'no' to my hand or is that a 'no' to going to see the swing and Tommy's work? I held up the end that he put in big bolts to tie onto the chains."

She stood up. Took the hair brush to the bathroom and laid it bristles up on the counter. Patted her hair and started braiding her long tresses.

When she came back, she said, "let's go".

He waited, "Sigmund Freed made up all kinds of words. My ID is working overtime. Do you know what ID means? After a long pause, he said, "Nevermind. As Bella would say, it wouldn't be 'seemly' for me to visit with you near that bed".

They left. He opened the door for her and waited. She went out into the hall and kept going. With the door quietly closed, he followed. They went out the twisted back screen door. With her head shaking, she said, "What a mess. Didn't know wind could do this much or cause this much trouble".

"Those jeans are a good fit", he said.

She turned and walked backward. Careful to watch for loose gravel. Kept her head down. Looked puzzled but said nothing. He followed, smiling at the shy girl who wanted his company but wouldn't admit it.

The swing was fixed. Tommy was gone. "Oh my! Tommy did such a good job!"

"yes, he did. Shall we test it?"

They gingerly sat down. She at one end, be at the other. With a loose coat, he put it on the hand rail. His other hand rested on the back of the swing as he got comfortable.

"Why did you come back?" she asked shyly.

"Well, because I wanted to talk to you", he said.

"Me?"

"yes, you".

Silently, they began to gently push the swing. Without any preamble, she said "Amee..."

Interrupting... he said", Amee has this place. She still loves her husband, and she now has you. What do you want, or need, little one?"

"Just...I don't..." She kept shaking her head. Suddenly she sat straight and moved away from the edge of the swing away from him. Mama musta say and the least of them shall lead them or something like that. Mama's gone. The future won't... it won't stand still! But

everybody has a place. This is a good place. It's Amee's place. Even...
" She became quite again.

Softly, Mr. Fields said, "Even who? Were you thinking about someone else? Maybe someone who was important to you?"

"No. About places. You have a place, don't you, Mr. Fields?"

He laughed. Then moved a bit closer.

"Sure. Lots of places. But none as important as where you are. I need to know you are warm and dry, eating well, sleeping safe, and away from those who want to hurt you. Are you happy here?"

"Woulda, Shoulda, Wanta. Wishes or wants. Oughta... What chances do they have, I wonder", she said out of the blue. "Amee calls you Ed. That must be your other name. Bet your main place is where Bella is." She was quiet again. "Listen! I heard something."

She jumped up. Ran to the barn. It's Mr. Gregory! Hurry. We need to see what's wrong!!

He was slow to follow. Shook his head, grabbed his coat and followed her to the barn.

Mr. Gregory was restless, turning around and kicking at the straw under his feet. The half-door to his stall was still latched.

Blondie talked nonsense to him to try to ease his restless spirit.

"Oh my. Amee forgot to feed him. She must be really out of... let's see. Where do I look for food. Don't know! Hafto remember. Ugh, ugh, ugh". She patter her forehead with her open hand. Turned round and round. This must be what you want. "Mr. Fields pointed to a large wooden box beside the door with a bucket and divider. Inside was two kinds of feed.

She ran to the big box. Scooped one kind of grain into the bucket then ran to dump it into Mr. Gregory's leather feed satchel fastened to the wall just inside his stall." Hunger does strange things to humans, too". She said to the horse. "here is what you need -----maybe". She went back to the big box near Mr. Fields. Looked up at him, then got the other small bucket from the second side. Filled the second bucket and ran back to the horse and dumped the second bucket of feed. She had to push Mr. Gregory's head aside to put the other feed into his pouch.

"There now. That should do. I'll find an apple if I can. Calm down. You'll be alright." Slowly, she walked away. Mr. Fields was leaning on the door, post, smiling. She went toward him with the small bucket in her hand. Pitched it in the box and dusted off her hands.

"You sure are efficient", Mr. Fields said. Puzzled, Blondie just stared. "Don't know how Amee could... whatever".

She looked back at the horse. "He seems okay now", she said.

"Let's leave him to enjoy his dinner. Speaking of which, have you eaten?"

She shook her head. "Don't know how to cook. Know how to do leftovers in the microwave, though. Want to see what we can find. It's okay with me."

He wiped a hand over his face to hide a laugh. Shook his head, grinned, and said, "okay. Let's go look!"

Back at the house, he straightened the damaged door so they could go through it more easily. Then he sat at one of the straight back chairs at the kitchen table. His coat dangled from the back of the chair he had chosen.

"First, I'll go check on Amee. It's not like her to sleep so long."

She stuck her head through Amee's door, Blondie didn't want to make any noise if possible. Still in her work clothes, Amee was hard asleep.

Blondie noticed a pirce of paper in Amee's hand. She moved close to the sleeping woman. Scribbled on the paper was something hard to read. Her sleeping face was too tight and much too pale.

She flew out of the room to find Mr. Fields still sitting at the table.

Trembling, she barely said, "Please come. I think... I think some-thing is wrong". She turned away, went to the counter to hold on then said, "Something is not right. Please..."

Jumping up, Mr. Fields went to her, "What's the matter?"

A head shake was the only answer he got. "Something... you will know. I don't know but... come, please." She tried to reach for him but drew back. Shivered some more. Put her arms around herself then walked woodenly back to Amee's room.

He followed.

She leaned against the wall beside the door when he went inside Amee's room. She did not see him bend over her and touch the side of Amelia Margot's neck, nor did she see him shake his head or cover her with the throw that lay over her feet.

With the torn piece of paper in his hand, he found Blondie with her arms still wrapped around her middle and shivering. She knew without being told.

He covered her shoulders with his arm and hand. "Let's go into the living room. There are many things to do but we can't do anything here. Come with me". He guided her to an overstuffed chair. Waited for the shivering to slow down then stood by the desk trying to decipher the scrawls on the piece of paper he held.

"Try this. You may be able to figure it out. I can't". He handed the scrap of paper to her.

"I don't know", she said without looking.

"Look at it please. Try to make out what it means".

She looked at the paper, then she looked at him. Back at the paper. Back to him.

She finally studied the paper, turned it every direction then said, "ok means... I think... check and 'dsk' means desk...maybe. She may mean 'living room by putting R near dsk'. I don't know". She fluttered both hands as she let the paper fall to the floor. She sat shaking her head. "I don't know. I don't know. I don't know". She kept on repeating.

He looked around the room. A small flip top desk set under a tall window near the wall to wall bookcases. That must be what she meant. He lowered the flip top to find cubicles and drawers.

He opened every drawer to find paper clips and various stuff that belongs in a desk, the cubicles held envelopes, bills, statements, and personal notepapers. In the lower part of the desk drawers, he found insurance forms, statements and legal papers on the farm, the car, the various equipment and on the house.

Tired, he was about to give up. On top of a thin packet, he found a letter from her doctor. A small hand touched his back.

"I don't know what to do", she said as he turned around. "Do you know what to do?" she asked then went back to her chair to sit while shaking her head.

"First", he said, "I'll call the doctor. Then, we will wait for him. I need to call Bella. Maybe after the doctor comes. Meanwhile, I'll look at the packet. I'll put it back where it was, if it is a will. He glanced through the first page in the packet. He then sat down across the cold fireplace from Blondie and put his hands on either side of his head.

"There is a lot to do", he said and did nothing.

After a long time of silence, he bounded up, took his phone from his pocket, walked to the desk again to get the letter from the doctor and punched in the doctor's number.

They talked as he walked down the hall, not wanting her to hear his side of the conversation.

Next, he called his own house to talk to Bella. After their long conversation, he said, "tomorrow is soon enough". Bella moaned and moaned. "I'll call... or you can call me when you know about what time you will be here. No. There's nothing you can do until then. Yes, I'll be close by".

He went back to the living room. To Blondie who still sat and stared into space. He sat but said nothing for a long while.

They heard a car door slam. Both jumped up. He went to the front door and opened it. The doctor got his bag and rushed up the front steps.

She stood still. He motioned to the doctor to come in and to follow him down the hall. Blondie sat down and twisted her hands in knots in her lap. She waited nervously.

Voices carried from down the hall as the two men returned.

"She knew this could happen and told me as much as she knew". She wanted to lay beside her husband on the back forty of this farm. They were very happy here. Somewhere there is Platt of the property. I'll call the family lawyer if you'd like. Here is this. You'll need to make copies. She couldn't hear Mr. Field's response. He musta said something. The doctor nodded in her direction when he left.

Mr. Fields came into the living room. Instead of sitting down, he paced back and forth and put paper.

On the kitchen table, there were two salads with chopped tomatoes, cucumbers, sliced ham, cheese, and something else she didn't know. Forks lay on a cloth napkin next to the salad bowls.

"Tea is sweet, or if you want it, there's plenty of milk." Amelia Margot pulled out a chair and started to eat.

Blondie stood still and looked around. Finally, she sat down and peeked under the cloth that was in a basket on the table. Sure enough. The bread was there. Cut thick, it looked home-made.

"The salad came from the garden. Washed and chopped, everything in it tastes good. I put a bit of oil and vinegar on it to bring out the flavors. The white pieces on top are pieces of chopped chicken, in case you wondered. We can gather eggs after our naps if you want to."

"Gather eggs? Do they grow on bushes? Never ever heard of such a thing. Gather eggs! Huh!" Blondie picked at the salad with her fork, confused. After a while she said, "More bread. . .please?"

"Bread? It's in the basket. Help yourself. After lunch, we'll rest before we go to the hen house to gather the eggs. The hen house is the shed near the barn." She had intentionally ignored Blondie's statements about 'gathering' eggs, figuring she'd find out in the fullness of time.

"Near the big tree? Yes!" She began to eat the salad. "Okay," she said as she tucked her head down. "Good!" she quietly muttered, her mouth full.

"I will rest now," Amelia Margot said. Using her cane, she took her empty bowl and her fork rinsed them and put them in the dishwasher beside the sink. The room with the bath you are familiar with. That room can be yours. See you later."

Blondie mimicked Amelia Margot's acts with her now empty bowl and fork. After she put them in the dishwasher, she washed her hands and dried them with the cloth that lay near the sink.

Going down the long hall with doors on both sides, she saw Amee stretched out in the room with the first door. There was a rail fixed to the bed next to her. "Must need it to keep her from falling out. That bed is sure high." Blondie was trying to be quiet and mumbled to herself.

Extra clothes were still thrown across the bed where they had been left after the turban fitting and the cuff fixing. Blondie carefully hung up all the shirts that still had hangers on them and found a drawer with pants in it where she put the unworn jeans.

"I'll put the damp towel on the rod-thing in the bathroom, but don't know what to do with the others. Oh well. Guess I'll just get under the fancy spread and rest if'n I can."

She turned back the bedspread and crawled under it. Before she knew it she was asleep, talking to herself. "Can't believe this is so soft..."

"Unlatch the opening." Amelia Margot pointed at the wooden turn that held the chicken coop closed.

"This thing? Am I supposed to turn it or am I supposed to pull on it? I never been to a chicken house before. Mama kept her chickens outside. Mama's gone, you know."

They had gone beyond the big tree to the small shed filled with stack upon stack of laying hens.

"Just turn it. The tall door will open. There! You did it! Now. Carefully reach in and gather the eggs. They are under the chickens. Go slowly the hens may try to peck."

Scared to try, Blondie watched Amee's hand come out from under the plump red laying hen with two brown eggs. She lay them in the cloth bottomed basket that Blondie held.

"Thanks. I'll take the basket and you can gather the eggs this time." Blondie hugged herself and shook her head. Oh come on! You can do it! Try it. Just move slowly. That's good. You can do all sorts of things!"

"Like gather eggs? Yeah. I guess." Blondie lay a brown egg in Amee's basket before she smiled and danced up and down.

"Hey! Just look at you! Okay. Get one more and you can go swing. Will that be alright?"

"One more. One more is all I need to get? Then I can go swing? Okay!" Cautiously, Blondie reached under the placid fat hen. Careful not to get pecked, she felt two eggs. She stopped to look at Amee then took them both out.

"Lookee! Got two! Take them. Don't know." Her hands were shaking.

Amee took both eggs and said, "Good, good, good. Now, go swing." Amee went back toward the house laughing. "When I get back, we'll go pick some runner beans. That is, if you have had enough swing time." With the basket on one arm, she walked slowly helped along by her cane.

"Beans? Running? Never knew beans could run. Oh well." Blondie grinned and swung with her bare toes sticking out of her almost new high-cuff jeans.

"Sure are some funny words around here. Guess I better be glad that there's nobody stealing or hittin' on folks. At least it's not raining. And there's a swing. Wheee"

Inside, Amelia Margot sat at the kitchen table and cut an insole to put inside Blondie's sneaker. She added enough white glue to make sure the insole stayed in place.

"There. That should work until I figure out what else to do."

Once the glue dried, she walked slowly to the swing with the pair of sneakers in one hand and her cane in the other. She held them out. Blondie stopped swinging.

"They're white! Never knew they were white!"

Laughing, Amelia Margot said, "They are just washed and dried. I'm not sure I fixed the hole or that they still fit. You can try them on now, if you like."

Blondie scooted off the swing and took the sneakers. They fit. When she looked up again, she noticed Amee's apron tied around her slender waist but with the many long pockets.

"What's all the pockets about? Mana's apron had pockets on it, but they were'nt as long as yours."

"Let's go get some beans, tomatoes, and some corn for supper. I'll make some fried chicken and some cornbread. How does that sound?"

"Yumn! Are they runner beans? Where will we find such stuff?"

"You'll see. This way." She laughed as they headed back toward the house. "We'll walk behind the flowers. There's a walkway back there. We'll follow the walkway. That's where my garden grows. I like to see how it is growing from the side porch or the kitchen."

"You have tall roses in the front, like Bella. These are short flowers but I don't know what their names are. Everything or everybody has a name. I remember Sam. He was tall. Barry was short because he had his legs off from his knees down. No feet. Couldn't handle curbs."

Blondie got quiet and stayed solemn for a few minutes. They walked on.

"These are Gerber daises. Those are geraniums, these are called Baby's Breath sometimes. At other times, or in other countries, they have a different name. Behind them is the garden." Amelia Margot explained.

Blondie brightened and pointed. "Are those the beans? They're trying to run up that bunch of string." She laughed.

"Pick some. I'll carry them in one of my pockets. That's good. Twist off the fullest. Leave the little ones to grow some more. When you think we have enough for both of us, let's get two or three small tomatoes that are red enough to taste good."

They continued to fill the deep pockets before they moved on to the corn. "How do you know when to get the corn? It's hiding."

"Look at the tassels. If they are brown, the corn is ripe."

"What in the world are 'tassles'? You mean like on a hat? Don't see any hats around here. Could sure use one to keep the sun from burning the top off my head, though."

Amee laughed. "I guess the corn tassels are a bit like a hat. Just look at the top of the fattest ears of corn. If the silky stuff sticking out is brown, twist off the ears and we can have one each for supper."

"I never knew food grew in the ground." She thought it strange and shook her head. "What do they do when it rains"

"They like water. Makes their roots grow."

"Roots? Do I have roots? I'd like something to drink right now. Can't find anything fit to drink sometimes."

With her hands on her chin and her feet on the rounds of the chair, Blondie sat at the table, away from the busy Amee who mixed cornbread and shoved it in the oven, fried chicken in a deep iron skillet and steamed beans over small potatoes. She had kept the small potatoes in a bag behind one of the doors in the cupboard.

"It's a feast. Who else is coming, I wonder," said Blondie.

"If you will," interrupted Amee, "take the bean stems out to the back and put them in the compost box. It is in the end of the garden. You'll see it."

Slowly, Blondie got up. She picked up the metal bowl with the bean stems and bent out the screened door, mumbling. "No con-crete. No getting lost all the time, No fights by bad . . .but soft beds, lotta good stuff, plenty to eat even though it is strange, may as well. . . Suddenly, she whirled and danced.

"Now. Where is that box? Cornbread must have corn in it. Sure smells good! Oh, there it is. In you go, bean stuff." She hurried to run back inside to see Amee put plates on the table.

"I'll put the spoons and forks on the table if you will show me where they are."

"In the drawer on the table. It's on my side. Look and you will find them." She went to peek in the oven. "Almost done. Please hand me a plate for the cornbread."

"I don't know where to look for plates." She opened a cabinet. "Oh. There they are." She got three plates. One for the cornbread and two for each of them.

"You are quick." said Amee. "Soon we will eat."

Blondie sat obediently and waited. Finally, she said, "Who else is coming? There must be somebody else, there is so much here, you can feed a whole bunch of folks. It a feast! Is anybody else coming?"

Amee laughed. "I don't like to cook all the time. So, we will have leftovers for some of the meals."

"Leftovers." Blondie kept saying 'leftovers.' All of a sudden, she put down her fork and said, "Am I a 'leftover'?"

Amee was busy cutting her chicken and did not hear what she said. "What?" She asked. "I didn't hear you. I was too busy cutting."

With a head shake, Blondie said more clearly, "Nothing. This is good. Afterwards, we'll have a nap, yes?"

"After we clean up the mess in here, yes." Amee nodded her approval.

"I'm the mess." Blondie mumbled as she finished eating and pushed her plate away. She looked at Amee who was finished too.

Amee stood up. "Let's clear away and clean up," she said.

Blondie watched and followed every step of the clearing away and the cleaning up. "I can do this and I can do many more things." Soon, she was helping. They both laughed at how much she was helping as they went down the long hall to their rooms.

Blondie slipped under the bedspread full dressed. She'd kicked off her tennies and fluffed up the pillow. "Soft," she whispered as she sighed and drifted off to sleep.

It was dark. She ran. Kept running. Couldn't find any end to the tunnel she was in. Feet were pounding behind her. She turned. Couldn't see. Kept running. Twisted against something. Someone was there. Fought. Hit, Kicked. Screamed.

She sat up with sweat streaming down her face. Somebody was really there. Oh. It's Amee.

Amee had something in her hands as she stood near the open door. "I brought you some things to sleep in." Amee tossed the bundle she had brought on top of the low chest near the door and left.

"A dream. It's only a dream," Blondie said as she wiped her face. Trembling, she looked around. "Looks like a war zone in here. Everything is out of place. I am out of place. Things are supposed to have their own place. Where is my place? Do I even have a place? Don't know."

She picked the bedspread up off the floor while she mumbled "This was. . . is. . . was a good place. No more bundling up to sleep on concrete and watch out for bad folks who only want to do bad things. No more rain or worse in my face. No more wondering when or what to eat. No more trying to find my way when I don't know where I am!"

She tried to untangle the sheets. Finally sat on the floor and gave up. With her arms on her knees, she sat, held her head, and cried.

She heard voices. They sounded like they were coming from the house. She sat up, wiped her face, and began to move. Voices were louder. She ran toward the bathroom.

As soon as she could, she straightened her hair, redid her braid and re-tied her torn plaid ribbon. When she ran down the hall, she said to herself, "He came back!"

She slowed down as she reached the kitchen. Mr. Fields was there but he was holding Amee. Her head was on his shoulder. His arms were around her. They parted when he saw Blondie who had turned to leave.

"Wait!" he called. She walked stiffly through the front room on her way to the hall. He tried to follow her but bumped into a chair.

Amee found her way to the front of the sink. She dried her tear-stained face on a clean hand towel.

Angry, Blondie stomped her foot, turned, and said, "I thought you came for me! But no! You came for another reason. Well, good! Have your privacy. I am fine!"

He stopped and shook his head. Relaxed now and smiling, he said, "Do you realize that is the longest and finest sentence you have ever. . .it was wonderful! Do you know that you have not hit nor patted your head even once? Please don't be made at me. I did come. I came to see both of you. Amelia Margot was frightened. You were. . . what happened?"

She turned her back to him, still rigid with anger. "It was just a dream! I had a dream."

In the living room, he sat on the sofa. "Please, sit down. Tell me about it. What kind of dream did you have?" Relief showed in his voice. He patted the seat beside him to urge her to sit.

Blondie looked around. She finally chose a straight chair near the fireplace. She sat with her head down and twisted her hands together, waiting on him but embarrassed for herself. Eventually, sha said half-aloud, "It was only a dream."

"But you were screaming," he countered. "Tell me what you were dreaming, please."

A deep sigh from her followed his request. She waited and was hesitant to begin. After a few minutes, she began slowly.

"It was dark. I ran and ran and ran. There were some folks who wanted to hurt me. It was dark. I was running. Then there was fighting but I don't know where I was. The dark was all around. That's what I remember mostly."

Her head was still down. Her hands twisting air.

"You don't know who it was that you were fighting? You don't know where you were? Could you have been back on the streets? Could you have been afraid to stay here? Who could you have been fighting?"

"I don't want to run! I don't ever want to fight anybody for anything! I don't want to try to sleep when somebody's after me to hurt me. I don't want to have to beg for food. It's hard!" She tried not to cry. "But you. . . you came. . .you held. . ." She stood up and paced. "I don't

know."

He stood up and smiled as he went to her and put his hands in his pockets so he wouldn't touch her.

"Stop saying. you don't know. Of course, you know. You are very bright and very capable. You are shrewd about how to survive in every, or any, situation. You have a place in the world. The question is, do you want this place?" He stood there helpless to know what to say or to do. At long last, he said, "Answer me!"

She wrung her hands. Held her head. "Okay! The answer is yes. . . but. . ."

Amee was standing in the doorway with the towel in her hands. "But what?" She quietly asked.

"I want to tell you something you may not know," Amee said. She stood but held on to her cane. "When my husband died, Mr. Fields came to his funeral. They were friends, but it was the first time I had met Eddie. My George knew everybody in the county, but I didn't. When you fought and screamed over and over, I didn't know what to do. So, I called the first person I thought of who might understand. Mr. Fields was in the area on business anyway, so he came here to check on both of us."

Amee knelt beside Blondie who was shaking and hugging herself as she looked at first one then the other.

"It was a natural reaction that he hugged me when he saw that I was crying and scared. Besides, I didn't know what to think when I went in your room to take those night clothes. You were wild! I ran!"

Blondie seemed to shrink inside herself. She only said, "Sorry. Didn't mean to scare you." Since she didn't know what else to do, she hunched her shoulders, put her hands under her chin in what looked like a prayer, and kept repeating, "Sorry. Sorry." She also kept bumping her hands together under her bent head.

He said, "You never answered my question."

Blondie raised her head. "What. . .what was it?"

"It had something to do with your wishes and wants. I don't quite remember." He paused and scratched his head. As he smoothed down his hair, he said, "Oh, yes. Now I know. I asked whether you could see yourself being here. I mean, all the time. If you had three wished, tell me what you'd wish for." He talked in a hurry without giving her time to answer or a chance to talk.

"You must want to run away from someone. Maybe there is a place you are trying to run from. What is it, or who is it you desperately want to leave? It may be a place or it may be people. Please help us understand what you want or need." Finally, he stopped.

Blondie kept shaking her head and wringing her hands. "Don't know." She almost whispered. Then, she got still and quiet as she sat straighter and taller.

"Yes," she said as she look back and forth to each of the most important people she knew. "Yes. Yes. And yes. This is. . . this can be . . . I want this to be my place." She hurried to finish. Afraid of what she was saying, she

Seemed fearful of forgetting the words she wanted.

"Everybody has a place. I don't want to go back to those places where I've been. Those are too hard. Please,

can I make a place. . .this is a good place. . . the food is good here, I'm not hungry here. . . Okay?. . . Sorry I scared anybody. I'll try to learn. . .please? Okay?" She seemed to shrink into herself again.

Amee and Mr. Fields looked at each other. Both nodded. Both were ready to leave the past behind.

"If you have any more bad dreams, call me," Amee said. "You don't have the fight or be afraid any more. If Mr. Fields is in this area, he can check on both of us. Is that okay with you?"

The phone rang in Mr. Field's pocket. He fished it out and went into the kitchen, saying, "Excuse me," to the women folk.

"What?" he said. "Yes. I know. Got sidetracked." He looked at his watch. "Okay. I'll be there is fifteen or twenty minutes. Try not to get your knickers in a twist."

He hung up, stuffed the phone back into his pocket, and went into where the girls were sitting. "Sorry. I have to go now. Is everything okay here?"

"Yes." Amelia Margot said. She looked at Amy and got a nod. "We're fine. I'll see you out."

They left together. Blondie watched them go. She covered her face with both hands and sobbed.

CHAPTER 13

TOMMY

He knocked. Without waiting for an answer, he opened the screened door to the porch and went into the kitchen.

Amelia Margot was turning over bacon strips in a black wrought iron skillet. A medium stack of fluffy pancakes set on the back of the old-fashioned stove to stay warm. She kept turning when Tommy appeared. "Hi, Tommy," she said.

"Mama sent me over with this little box of rolls she made from scratch. Said you might be willing to trade some 'maters for 'um. Our 'maters got the blight. All squishy and go them big brown spots all over. Not fit for nuthin exceptn' maybe some hog feed. Here's a sack if''n you're willin'."

Tommy rattled away while Amelia Margot finished with the bacon. She put it on a paper to drain and picked up a dry cloth to wipe her hands.

"Sure, Tommy. How is you mother these days?" Without waiting for his answer, she said, "Blondie's out back. She's getting some eggs so we can have scrambled eggs with our pancakes and bacon. I thought we had plenty of eggs but then I had to bake a cake." She went to one of the tall cabinets.

"The cake needed some six eggs, so we ran out. Here, please take half of it for you, your mother and your sisters. Is your dad out of town? Be sure to give your mom the first piece. Okay?" She wrapped the red velvet cake in waxed paper and gently set it on a spare plate to be put on top of the tomatoes.

"Here's a spare cabbage. Let's put it in the bottom of your bag so the soft things can go on top. If your mother decides to make soup, a cabbage leaf makes all kinds of soup very flavorful. I'm sure she already knows that."

She lay the bag down. "Oh. Here comes Blondie. She lives here now."

Blondie waited for Tommy to move out of her way. She stared at his dirty bare feet while she held the egg basket carefully so as not to drop it or to let him bump it.

"I got four egg, Amee. I hope that's enough."

"That's fine. I'll put this cloth here. You can put the eggs on it so they won't roll off and break. Tommy here brought some rolls. Please go with him to the garden and get five or six plump ripe tomatoes. If you twist them, they should come off their vines very easily. That was there is no need to squeeze them."

As she talked, Amelia Margot took off her apron and tied it around Blondie. "This will keep your hands free while you pick. Just use the pockets to put the tomatoes in. We'll put them in Tommy's bag to carry home with him.

On the was to the garden, neither said anything. All of a sudden, Tommy, who was walking behind Blondie, said, "You sure are pretty!"

Blondie stopped. She turned around. "And you sure are dirty!" They stared at each other.

"Come on. Let's get something in these pockets so I can go eat!" She turned and went to the tomato patch as she bossed him. Soon she felt too guilty and knew she needed to make peace even though she was not sure how to go about it.

"You do know your colors don't you? You point out the red ones and I'll pick 'em." She was too hungry to think about peace.

"Of course I know red when I see it! Just 'cause I can't read don't mean I don't know colors." He stomped on. "Here's some," he hollered.

She twisted the tomato from its vine and put it in a pocket that almost touched the ground when she bent over. "Do you ever wear shoes?" she asked as he pointed and she twisted.

"Out growed 'em. Besides, I'm tough. Don't need 'em. That 'nough 'maters. I need to be gettin' on back."

"I can read, you know. Lets go find some runner beans before you go. They are good!"

As they went on to the bean patch, she gently asked, "Why can't you read? You're big enough." She held the apron up with one hand, and patted her forehead with the other hand as she wondered about the boy who was almost as tall as she.

They found ripe beans, fat and ready to be picked. The beans were almost head high. They pulled and picked until a pocket was filled. Then they went back to the house.

He finally said, "Don't know. All the letters keep moving around. Sometime or other, somebody will figure out how to settle them letters in one place so folks can do book learning. Till then, I'll just fix stuff. I can fix just 'bout anything."

"Have you tried?"

"Tried! Huh! Everybody's tried, including me! It don't matter no more. I'm not goin' back anyhow. "

Before they reached the screened porch, Blondie stopped. He almost bumped into her but stepped back to look at the wind blowing her hair around.

"Back where?" She asked.

"To that school, you ninny. Just cause they make fun of me don't mean I'm stupid." He got madder and madder as he thought about it.

He repeated, "Not going back. I can fix things. So what if they tell me I have to go until I'm sixteen or so. They can't keep on doing no good and lettin' me be bigger than all those little kids who read them books. I won't go, that's all. Let's go in!'

They went inside to give their pickings to Amelia Margot so she could pack the tow-sack he'd brought. The cake went on top.

"There. She said as she handed him the sack. Can you manage this? It's heavy."

"Umnnn. That cake sure smells good. Thanky. Thanky. Thanky. Yes'um. Sure appreciate all this stuff. Bye." He left the two women standing.

"I can read." Blondie blurted out.

"Sure you can. Now sit while I scramble these eggs. We will eat soon."

They ate in silence.

Suddenly Blondie said, "Tommy's broken, too."

Amee's head went up and her fork was laid down.

Quietly, she said, "Broken? What do you mean, broken?"

Blondie answered, "Everybody's broken. I'm broken because I can't remember things. You are broken because you can't walk much without you cane. Tommy's broken because he can't read. We're not the only ones broken."

Amelia Margot took her last bite. She lay down her fork and propped her elbows on the table. She slowly said, "It's not what we can't do that's important. It is who we are and what we can do that counts. Can you see that?"

"No." Blondie shook her head. "Some folks are important. They have big titles, or bib houses, or maybe even both. Others THINK they are important and try to bully folks. No. I can't see what you are saying. Things are just the way they are. You must mean something else."

They both sat quietly.

"I found a baby girl once." Blondie shifted her weight. "She was throwed away." She put her head down and shook it. "I sound like Jimmy... No. More like Tommy. I'll start over. "I found a little girl baby who wasn't important. She was *thrown* away." Quiet again, Blondie rested her head on both hands.

Amelia Margot didn't know what to say. So, she said nothing. After a long while, she spoke.

"When my dear husband died, at first I was angry. I was so mad all I could think of was how dare he go off and leave me! I kept asking him that even though he was not around to hear me. Then I'd cry. It took me a long time to realize that he was gone and the fact was that he was not going to be here any more. I still miss him.

But this is going to be the way things are going to be. It was what it was. It is what it is."

"Was he important?" Blondie asked.

"To me he was. Isn't that enough to make somebody important? It is the same reality thing with you now. You are important to me. So. That makes you important! Now. Let's go see if there is feed for the horse. There has been so much going on around here, I may not have left him enough to eat! Let's go."

Bewildered, Blondie followed her. "A horse? Didn't know there was a horse!"

Amee hurried as best she could. On the way out, she grabbed a sweater that was hanging on back of the kitchen door. She shrugged it on as they left. Apples were in a basket on the long table. Laying her cane down a minute, she finished putting on the sweater and the pocketed an apple. "Now. Are we ready to go?"

Blondie went behind her asking as many questions as she could think of.

"Do you get up early to feed him? It must be a 'him' is it? Do you ever let him out? Does he have a name? Where do you keep him? Why haven't I ever heard him make any noise? I never saw a horse around anywhere."

Out of breath, they reached the big barn. "Why did I not know you had a horse?"

Amee laughed. "I get up a lot earlier than you. That's when I feed him and let him walk around a bit. I used to ride him. Do you want to ride him some? His name is Mr. Gregory. He likes gentle people."

A slow nod of her head gave her Blondie's answer but she wasn't sure about riding since she had never seen any horses except those the police rode around on sometimes.

"There's a blanket and saddle in the next stall. You can get the bridle, the blanket and the saddle. I can't get the saddle any more but he needs a good ride. That is, if you want to."

Amee turned on the overhead light that flooded the whole area in order for Blondie to see what she needed to bring into Mr. Gregory's stall.

"Come on. He won't hurt you." Amee stroked Mr. Gregory's neck and whispered to him.

Timidly Blondie walked toward the rear stall and came closer to where Amee was with the big horse that was sprinkled with white patches.

"Don't know. Don't know how." She said and plucked at her braid.

The horse stood patiently as Amee fixed a harness over his head. She mumbled quietly to him as he came forward. Blondie backed away.

"Here. Hold the reins."

The horse shook his head. Afraid, Blondie grabbed the reins and backed up some more. Mr. Gregory followed her. Amee laughed. She took an apple out of her sweater pocket.

"He likes apples. Don't be afraid. He won't bite anything but the fruit. You can go get the saddle now. I'' hold the reins while you put on the saddle. Okay?"

Blondie didn't know what to do, but she brought the saddle and just stood still with the heavy thing in both arms. Amee threw the blanket over the horse's back and reached in the next stall to get a fat stool that had two wide steps on it.

"Here. Put one of the stirrups, these will do, in the saddle and then put the saddle on top of the blanket. I'll help if I can."

The stirrup fell when the saddle went on. They both laughed at their struggle and at the long stirrups that hung on both sides of the horse. He neighed and slung his head. They both laughed more.

Between sniffling, snickering, and trying to keep her balance, Amee said, "Nobody knows how to do much the first time they try. You, however, can do a lot of things even when you don't know how! Let's get him tied and then let's get out of here."

"Tied? Tied how? What's that funny-looking stool for? Here, let me take it. Just tell me what to do next and we can go out to the fresh air. It is stuffier in here than it was. I thought we were going to feed him, not take all day and put all this stuff on him. Can we go out soon?"

"Okay. You're right. We can hurry along. If you are ready, put your arm under the horse and grab the wide belt. Fasten it under him tight. We'll guide him outside. Take the stool with you."

"What? You want me to put my arm under his fat belly? You've got to be kidding. Am I supposed to hold onto something while I'm under the biggest horse I've ever seen much less ever been close to?"

Blondie put both hands on her hips and stood firmly where she was.

"Use the saddle horn to grab hold of and step up onto the stool. When you put your left foot into the stirrup, you can sling your right foot over and sit in the saddle." Amee had ignored Blondie's outburst and given her instruction of how to get up on the horse instead.

"Go ahead. You can do it." Amee said.

Guessing what was the saddle horn, Blondie would not admit she didn't remember left from right. Instead, she moved the stool closer and put a foot in the stirrup. Over she went. Mr. Gregory seemed to understand that she was a newcomer.

"Wheee. I did it! What's next?" Out of breath, Blondie sat still. So did the horse.

"Here. Let me tighten the cinch that dangled beneath Mr. Gregory. "I'll cinch this for you. It's too loose. It'll keep things, including you, from falling off."

Blondie leaned over to see what Amee was talking about. She had to grab the saddle horn. She'd leaned too far and the saddle slid.

"Oh me. Guess you meant I might fall off the horse, huh?"

"Yes, you ninny. You might. There. It's done." Amee raised up from tightening the cinch and stepped away. She was laughing so hard she could barely stand without something to hold onto. She moved toward to swing and sat down, holding her sides.

"I have to sit for a minute. You can ride if you like. We'll put the stool away later." She sat on the swing. Blondie sat on the horse. The horse waited.

"What do I do now?"

Amee laughed some more while shaking her head. "I don't know." Between giggles and wiping her face from the tears that streamed down, she managed to say, "I guess you'll have to pretend you are in the swing and rock back and forth. He will go when he wants to go. Just wait until he is ready, I reckon."

Then, as if he heard her, Mr. Gregory went past the swing with his head held high. Sensing he had a new rider on board, he walked slowly then went back into the barn and all the way to his own stall.

"Stop. Please Mr. Horse! Wait! Stop! How do I get down? Stop! Wait!

Most of the way through the barn, Blondie shouted. Amee heard the calls.

Hobbling and laughing silently, Amee and her cane brought the stepstool to Blondie and stopped Mr. Gregory

Just before he went into his stall. "Throw you leg over. Hold the saddle horn and slide down. I'll catch you if you need me to. The stool should be in the right place for you to reach it. Come on now."

Blondie held on with one hand. She put the other hand on the back of the saddle as she got one leg over and slid. With one foot still in the stirrup, she knocked the stool over and landed on her bottom at Amee's feet.

She looked up to see Amee doubled over, laughing. Finally, Blondie laughed too.

"Whoa. That's an adventure," she said. "Wait until I tell Tommy. Bet he can't ride a horse!"

"Don't want to, either. Bet you can't drive a tractor!

Tommy stood at the entrance to the barn, leaning on an upright at the door. He stood straight and smiled at Blondie as she dusted off the seat of her pants and set the stool out of the way.

"Momma said to tell you thanky, Ms. Amelia Margot. She sent over some stuff for you what I left on the table on the screen porch. It's soup in case you want some. Gotta go now." He left, laughing. "Can't ride a horse! Huh!"

They brushed more straw off themselves. Amee put more feed into Mr. Gregory's trough and then they went to the barn door. As Amee fastened it, Blondie asked, "Tractor? What's a tractor?"

On their way to the house, Amee tried to explain. "Umm, well, it's a machine that farmers use for a lot of different things. Mostly they use tractors for plowing or moving away stumps or big rocks or stuff, I guess."

She opened the screened door and got the large Ball jar filled with soup. "Most farm boys start driving them when they are around seven years old." She poured the soup into a pan and washed her hands.

Blondie interrupted as Amee adjusted the heat.

"Guess they don't need a license at that age. How does he know how to drive a tractor if he can't read? His mama's too busy with her babies to show him. Doubt she knows how, anyway." Blondie washed he own hands and wondered aloud.

"There's leftover cornbread if you want some," was Amelia Margot's answer.

"Oh yes." Blondie got out two white bowls for the soup and found two soup spoons in the table drawer. "Cornbread is good! But what will Tommy do when he's full grown if he won't go to school now and he can't ever read? Will he have to sleep on the streets like. . . Oh my! I don't want to remember what that's like!"

After she ate some soup and drank some of her sweet tea, Amelia Margot hesitated and said thoughtfully, "Not everybody needs to go to school. Tommy may keep on fixing things. He bright and very good with machinery. Some of the people around here ask him to help with their combines or tractors or anything that doesn't run properly."

She paused to finish eating, then continued. "They pay him a bit for every job. Do you. . .do you know. . .   what. . .do you know about money?"

"Don't need to. Don't have any. Usta have to. . .Don't remember." Blondie ducked her head down over her bowl and kept eating.'

"That was then. This is now." Amee said as she got up and got a can from a cabinet. She set it on the table, got some coins from it and spread them out. "Tell me what each one of these are and what they represent, please."

Blondie quickly stopped eating. She touched every coin one at a time but said nothing. She straightened the bills and put the ones with the ones, fives with the fives then laid her hand on the small stacks to mash them down.

After a long pause, she picked up a quarter. "This is a quarter," she said. When she lay her hand on the bills, she said, "These are ones. These are fives."

"What are the fives and ones called?" Amee asked.

Puzzled, Blondie answered, "Ones or fives, maybe?

Bills? Don't know. Must be something."

"They are called 'dollars.' Each one is 'a dollar.' The fives are called 'five dollars.' And so on. Do you see?"

"I find these!" She smiled spritely and picked up a penny. "Barry had all kinds of tinkling money in his hat. He had some paper money crumpled up in his hat, too. Bought burgers. We ate. They were good. No burgers here. Cornbread instead! Um. Good!"

"Yes. Everybody needs money when they go out to eat. But first we need to know what value each piece of money has. What are these called?" Amee touched the nickels and dimes.

She shook her head and mumbled, "Don't know. Can't member."

Patiently, Amelia Margot said, "This is now. Now you can remember what you learn. We will give up old ways and old days. They are no more. You will remember, okay?'

She sat straighter. Then she said, "Five dollars, one dollar, a nickel, a penny, a quarter. Today is a new day. Oops. I meant to say, a new 'way', hafta repeat them again." She repeated each one aloud and then did them over silently.

Amee clapped her hands, "That is very good." She left the coins on the table while she stuffed the bills in the can and returned it to the cabinet. "Those are for you. You have earned some money today."

"Me? I have money? Why do I need money? What good is it around here?"

"You earned it! Good! Keep it! I always pay for everything. Now. If you are finished eating, let's clean up the kitchen. Maybe we'll have more soup tomorrow evening."

"Tomorrow, tomorrow, I love you tomorrow." Blondie sang in a sweet but tight little voice then giggled and patted her forehead with her palm. She hummed as she carried the bowls and spoons to the sink. She suddenly blurted, "Bet Tommy didn't earn any money today. Bet he didn't learn how to saddle a horse either."

On the way down the hall, Amee heard her repeat, "Stirrup, Stirrup. Put one foot in each stirrup. Ha! Mr. Gregory is not as big as I thought he was at first. So there. Tommy can fix things, but so can I!"

In her new pajamas, she climbed under the bedspread and sighed. "Sure is soft. Can't have dreams that make me scared. Can't scream anymore. Just can't."

She thought she heard the phone ring as she drifted off.

Amee answered the call from Mr. Fields. She thought everything was going along well. Blondie seemed to have some improvement in her ability to remember. She wasn't sure and did not want to be too optimistic yet. Thanks were given for his checking on them both. "Come when you can." She said then hung up and slept.

"Tomorrow is today. Today is new. Hafta put down old ways. Now is now!"

Blondie talked to herself with her eyes still shut. "This bed is good! Sure beats concrete any old day or night."

Rain splattered the windows. Smells came from the kitchen. A bathroom was close. Food was handy and good. There was money (not much) in her pocket.

"Wow! She said. I'm not as broken as I usta be. Wonder where Barry--without any knees or feet--is now. Hope he's not getting wet!"

She took a quick bath, put on clean jeans and an almost new shirt and ran down the hall without shoes. Amee was stirring something.

"Morning! Can I. . .may I. . . help?"

Amee smiled and nodded as she held a bowl of steaming hot oatmeal on a saucer. There was a biscuit beside the oatmeal. "You know where the spoons are, right?"

"Unless they moved themselves, they are in the table drawer. I'll get them."

"Well. Aren't you frisky today! You mean you're not sore from bounding around on Mr. Gregory and taking a fall trying to get off? Must mean you've slept well."

"It's raining. So, what are we going to do today? I can read, you know."

"Read. That's a good idea. There are lots of books in the front room. If you'd like you can look through some of them or even take some to your room for later."

"Sam knows a lot. He knows a lot of people, too. Barry has to fight the curbs when he's on his platform. He had to have his legs taken off after he got bit by a shark, you know. He doesn't look like a seal but he says he's a Navy seal whatever they are." With a snicker, she finished her oatmeal and then stuffed a whole biscuit in her mouth.

Amee laughed, got up, then said, "It's best to take one bite at a time. Like we take one step at a time. Then, one day at a time. Okay. Let's clean up."

Blondie got the few remaining pieces of oatmeal that clung to her bowl and spoon, Took both to be rinsed and put into the dishwasher. She was gone is a flash to the front room and the books, singing, "All I want is a room somewhere with an enormous chair. . . "

Amee stopped to listen. She shook her head and slowly took off her apron before she went the same direction as Blondie.

Surrounded by books, they were on her lap, in the chair, on the floor, and lay sideways on the shelf. "Guess I know why Tommy can't read," she said as Amee came through the doorway. Can't make out these words. Must be in some other language." She handed one of the books to Amee.

"No wonder. These are some of my husband's old textbooks. He was a geologist. Taught all about rock and soils and other things. Some of the ones you have out are my old text books, too. They are all about why people do what they do. Sigmund Freud was the champion of psychos. He made up lots of words. One of his words is 'subconscious'. That's thoughts and memories we don't know about, but which guide us sometimes."

She got lost in some of the books before she gathered them up and put them back on the tall bookcase behind the overstuffed chair.

"Let's look at some with words you may know. They are over here. Amee moved to another bookcase. Blondie followed her and sat on a padded bench. "All these are plays. Some are. . ." Blondie interrupted.

"There's Shakespeare. 'To be or not to be.. '." She laughed. "Like me or Tommy. We don't know if we want to be or want not to be." She picked up one of the plays then put it back.

Amee didn't say anything. She just kept looking at the books. "Here are some by Mark Twain. His real name was Samuel Clements. He lived on the Mississippi River."

She was interrupted by "Mi-ssi-ssi-ppi. That spells Mississippi. Wonder why Tommy says the letters change places? It's a mystery." Blondie grew quiet and sat very still.

'These are mostly mysteries along here and below them are the fairy tales. Pick any that you want. I must go and do the outside chores now before the storm blows in and while the rain has stopped. You can explore to your heart's content." She left.

Blondie stood up. She ran her fingers over some of the book titles. "All this thinking makes my head hurt," she mumbled. She patted her forehead and left to go sit on the screened porch. With her back to the long table, she sat on the bench with her elbows on the table in back of herself. She thought about Tommy and that he was not going to school. "Wonder what not being able to read is like."

"I guess Amee took her rain hat and long checked raincost since they are not on the peg by the back door. She musta gone to the henhouse to gather some eggs. Don't know why I can't see her." She stood up and went to the back door. "I can at least look for her. No need to sit here like I'm broken! Ha! That's a good one. Must be broken! Wait! What's going on? All of a sudden, the sky is turning green and I can't find Amee. Better look harder. Rain is growing fierce!" Then she saw a crumpled mess.

Amee had fallen.

With her long braid only half done, Blondie ran into the down-pour. Amee's cane was too far away for her to reach it. She lay in a huddle with had basket of eggs protected by her raincoat.

"I'll take the eggs. Here is your cane. Can you get up if I get under one of your arms? Good going." Drenched, both began to hobble.

"The story shelter. We have to get to the storm shelter," Amee's voice was barely loud enough to be heard.

"I don't know where it is." Blondie tugged the muddy Amee who tried to wipe her face but made the muddy streak across her forehead that much bigger.

"This way. Behind the house. Let's go now. Hurry." They tried to run but couldn't. The wind was too strong.

At last, Blondie found the door to a storm cellar. It was closed but not locked and it was very heavy. "You have to pull the door really hard. It is not easy to open even when it is not raining."

Blondie tugged the heavy door open as best she could. Although Amee tried to help with the door but couldn't, she seemed to know where the steps were. The door slammed shut just as Blondie went inside. Pitch black darkness greeted them.

Amee found the two lanterns by feel. She handed one to Blondie. "Don't know how these work. Maybe you can figure it out. Never had to use them. Maybe they will light. Don't know."

"You sound like me." Blondie laughed. "I don't know, too. And fiddled with the lanterns.

Along with howling wing and a slamming porch door, they thought a voice called, "Let me in!"

"Here, Amee. Take the lantern. I'll try to push open that heavy storm door. Somebody's out there."

Using muscles she didn't know she had, Blondie pushed and grunted. Nothing budged. She turned around on the small platform close to the door and used her legs to push. The door opened a small crack.

Fingers gripped the door facing and pulled it wider. From outside, a small body dripping with rain, dived inside, and fell on top of Blondie.

Untangling arms and legs, she said, "Tommy. What are you doing outside in a storm? Get off me!" He rolled down the steps. Bumped into Amelia Margot holding two lanterns.

"S'cuse me, Ma'am. Sure is dark in here. You wonder why I'm here? Well, I was up at the next place over, helping get their tractor started. Didn't do no good. Motor's froze. Well, anyway. The big blow came up and they sent me on home. Didn't make it but remembered helping your husband dig this here shelter. I was a little kid then." He took a breath then continued. "So. Here I am. Sure is dark in here. Don't you have no lights Miss Amelia Margot?"

Amee handed the two lanterns to him.

Blondie added, "Since you are so good at fixin' things, see if you can make those lanterns work." She thought he bragged too much. Her impatience showed.

"Humn. Well. Their handles are kinda rusty. Must be battery run. How long have they been in here?"

Amee said, "I brought them in past week when I put watermelon pickles on the shelves. The batteries should still be good. Since I left the door open then, I don't know where their switches are, so I don't know how to turn them on."

He fumbled with both lanterns. One came on. The other one glimmered and then went out. "One has lost the button that went on the front. Maybe you can find it later."

He set the lanterns down. One was better than none.

"Boy! That wind is howling, Momma must be worried about me. I hope she and the girls are okay. Sure do."

They lost track of time. It was a long time, but not nearly as long as it seemed. Finally, both the wind and the rain let up. The door was opened and the three muddy, tense, damp and relieved were glad to be outside again.

Blondie still carried the basket of eggs.

Tommy half-ran behind Blondie, saying, "Thanky, for getting that door open. Gotta go." He too off. Amee turned off the lantern. She picked up her cane and slowly went up the steps Sadly, she said, "We'll look around later. First, we need to check on Mr. Gregory."

In the wind-whipped barn, Mr. Gregory stood in his stall, shivering. Amee took him an apple she had found on the ground then she covered him with an old blanket that had blown around a post in the barn.

She stroked his nose and hugged him while she whispered softly in his mane.

Blondie watched. She didn't know what to do.

On the way back to the house, they stopped to stare. Small and large limbs were everywhere along with leaves and whatever was not tied down.

"We can look for the swing later. First, we need to wash off some of the mud and change our clothes.

Blondie followed her, still numb. At the porch, they stopped. Almost all the screen wire was torn away from the uprights which were splintered or missing. The long table was outside. It rested on its top. The two long benches were scattered. One was on its top. The other was half way inside the porch and half way outside. It was tipped against the outside wall.

What was left of the screen wire was rolled up to the top of the rafters or was flapping in whatever breeze was left

"We can't do anything about anything just yet." Amee said. "Just be grateful it's a strong house."

The eggs sat on the counter, safe in the basket. They were left. The women walked like zombies to their own rooms to get rid of the mud. After warm baths and dry clothes, they were almost ready to go out again.

The Phone rang. Standing on the messy porch, Blondie heard he say, "He's fine. He's been in the storm cellar with us. He should be home any minute now. Are you and the girls safe? Your husband called? That's good. We'll talk later. Yes. I'm glad he made it home, too."

Blondie managed to set the big table upright and push it against the house. Amee shook her head as she came out to the porch.

"Let's go see about the garden," Amee said.

They went the back way, through a door that barely opened since it was held on only two broken hinged. Blondie helped Amee down the two concrete steps and followed her. Only stubs remained where one tomatoes grew. The stakes for running beams were scattered this way and that way or else they were broken off at ground level. A few stubborn beans clung to the vines ready to be picked. A few puddles rested where once something had been planted. The women were too shaken to do anything except look at the mess.

"Let's see about the hen house. There may be. . ."

Amee both wanted and didn't want to see anything else. She had worked so hard for so long, she was devastated.

"Oh, lookie. There is the swing. It's blown up on the . . . I don't know what that is. . .it is in the half shed that protects some kind of machinery. They are partly sheltered, I guess. I'll get the swing if I can. Oh, my. It's full of leaves."

She pulled and tugged but finally got the swing away from its resting place. "A car! There's a car! Does it still run? Oh, my. It looks pretty good. Can you drive it?"

Blondie prattled away. She brushed leaves away from the swing as she dug through the debris.

"I usta drive." Blondie patted her head then turned toward Amee. "That was then. This is now." She said as she lifted one end of the swing. "It's heavy. I can't do it by myself."

Amee smiled. "Yes. But we can do more later. Now it is time. . ."

"To see what all we need to do, right?" Blondie interrupted her. "One thing, then another. Right?"

" Right! But I think the saying is, f'irst one thing then another.' Something like that. " What shall we do first?"

"Eat left-overs?" That was the first real laugh Blondie has heard since Amee had fallen in the puddle and came up with half her face covered in mud. They hooked arms and laughing went back to the house to warm the left-overs.